big NATE OUT LOUD

Complete Your *Big Nate* Collection

big NATE OUT LOUD

by LINCOLN PEIRCE

Andrews McMeel
PUBLISHING®

Big Nate is distributed internationally by Andrews McMeel Syndication.

Andrews McMeel Publishing
a division of Andrews McMeel Universal
1130 Walnut Street, Kansas City, Missouri 64106

www.andrewsmcmeel.com

18 19 20 21 22 SDB 21 20 19 18 17

ISBN: 978-1-4494-0718-6

Library of Congress Control Number: 2011920757

Made by:
Shenzhen Donnelley Printing Company Ltd.
Address and place of production:
No.47, Wuhe Nan Road, Bantian Ind. Zone,
Shenzhen China, 518129
17th Printing – 7/16/18

These strips appeared in newspapers from
April 2, 2007, through November 4, 2007.

Big Nate can be viewed on the Internet at
www.gocomics.com/big_nate

For the Rhode Islanders

EVER SINCE MARCUS STARTED WEARING THROWBACK HOCKEY JERSEYS, EVERYONE'S DOING IT!

MARCUS IS A TREND-SETTER.
HEY, I'M GONNA DO THAT! I'M GONNA SET SOME TRENDS!

THAT'S NOT HOW IT WORKS! YOU DON'T DECIDE TO SET TRENDS!
WELL, THAT'S HOW NATE'S GOING TO DO IT!

PLEASE TELL ME REFERRING TO YOURSELF IN THE THIRD PERSON ISN'T A NEW TREND.
NOT A TREND, AMIGO. JUST THE WAY NATE ROLLS.
Peirce

IT'S OFFICIAL! I'VE DECIDED TO BECOME A TRENDSETTER!
WHAT'S THAT SUPPOSED TO MEAN?

IT MEANS I'M GOING TO **SET TRENDS**, OF COURSE! I'M GOING TO LIVE MY LIFE, AND PEOPLE ARE GOING TO **IMITATE** ME!

DUDE. PEOPLE AL**READY** IMITATE YOU.
THEY **DO**?

DOOYYY! GUESS WHO **I** AM!
SEE?
HA HA HA HA HEH HA
HA HA NICE HAIR! HA HA
Peirce

WHY SHOULDN'T I GET TO DETERMINE WHAT'S COOL?

WHAT THE...?
WHAT IS **THAT**?
IT'S A SOMBRERO, AMIGOS!

SOON EVERYBODY WILL COPY ME BY GETTING THEIR **OWN** SOMBREROS! IT'LL BE SOMBRERO MANIA! AND IT ALL STARTED WITH **ME**!

HEAR THAT, MARCUS? YOU'RE NOT THE **ONLY** TREND-SETTER AROUND!

YES HE IS!
NOW **THAT'S** A TREND I COULD GET BEHIND!
Peirce

MR. STAPLES! HOW'D I DO ON YESTER-DAY'S TEST?
GOOD TIMING, NATE! I'M JUST ABOUT TO CORRECT YOURS!

I'VE GOT A GOOD FEELING ABOUT THIS ONE!
YOU DO, EH?

MAY I ASK WHY?
UH OH.
Peirce

MR. GALVIN! WHAT DID I GET ON THE QUIZ?
I'M HANDING THEM BACK IN CLASS TODAY, NATE. YOU'LL FIND OUT THEN.

CAN'T YOU JUST GIVE ME A HINT OF HOW I DID?
OH, YOU PROBABLY HAVE A PRETTY GOOD IDEA OF HOW YOU DID.

NO, I DON'T! I HAVE NO CLUE!
SAY THAT AGAIN.

I HAVE NO CLUE?
THERE'S YOUR HINT.
Peirce

I LOVE THIS TIME OF YEAR! IT'S JOB-FREE!

JOB-FREE?
NO RESPONSIBILITIES, TEDDY!

THE SNOW HAS MELTED, SO THERE'S NOTHING TO SHOVEL...

THE GRASS HASN'T STARTED GROWING YET, SO THERE'S NOTHING TO **MOW**...

...AND THERE AREN'T ANY **LEAVES** ON THE GROUND, SO THERE'S NOTHING TO **RAKE**!

NO RESPONSIBILITIES! JOB-FREE!
WRIGHT

WHAT A REVOLTING TURN OF EVENTS.
DANG IT!

THAT WAS COACH CALLING. PRACTICE IS CANCELED BECAUSE THE FIELD IS TOO WET.
THAT'S TOO BAD.
POST

BUT JUST BECAUSE THERE'S NO PRACTICE...

...DOESN'T MEAN THERE'S NO BASEBALL!

...AND JUST BECAUSE THERE'S BASE-BALL DOESN'T MEAN THERE'S ATHLETIC ABILITY.
WHOOPS. SORRY.
Peirce

MOST PEOPLE THINK PITCHING IS ALL ABOUT ARM STRENGTH!

...BUT YOU'VE GOT TO USE YOUR LEGS WHEN YOU'RE A PITCHER!

...OR A CATCHER.
MY BAD!
Peirce

COME ON, NATE! LET'S PLAY CATCH!
AGAIN?

WE JUST PLAYED CATCH YESTERDAY!
I KNOW! BUT YESTERDAY I WAS THROWING MY SLIDER!

TODAY I WANT TO WORK ON MY SCREWBALL!

IT'S A SCREWBALL COMEDY, BUT NOBODY'S LAUGHING.
WHOOPS!
TRICKLE
TRICKLE
Peirce

NATE? HOW 'BOUT A LITTLE CATCH?
APR

LET'S GO, SON! THE BIG UNIT'S READY TO ROCK!

NATE! TIME'S A-WASTING!

STAY STILL... STAY VERRRY STILL.
OH, THERE YOU ARE!
Peirce

THERE YOU ARE, NATE! I'VE BEEN LOOKING FOR YOU TO PLAY CATCH!
OH. REALLY?

I'VE BEEN CALLING AND CALLING! I THOUGHT MAYBE YOU WERE TRYING TO AVOID ME! CHUCKLE!
ME? AVOID YOU? HA! HA! HA!

HA! HA! HA! HA! HA! HA! HA! HA!

I'VE GOT TO WORK ON MY CASUAL LAUGH.
Peirce

I CAN'T **TAKE** IT ANY-MORE! MY DAD KEEPS HOUNDING ME TO PLAY CATCH ALL THE TIME! WHAT IF I DON'T **WANT** TO PLAY CATCH?

WHAT DO YOU DO WHEN **YOUR** DAD ACTS LIKE THAT?
WELL, HE'S NOT INTO SPORTS, SO HE NEVER ASKS ME TO PLAY CATCH.

YOU'RE SO LUCKY, DUDE.
NOT REALLY.

HE MAKES ME GARDEN WITH HIM.
OUCH.
Peirce

WHAT'S UP, PEST?
THERE'S NOBODY TO PLAY CATCH WITH.

FRANCIS HAS A SWIM MEET... TEDDY IS VISITING HIS GRAND-PARENTS... NOBODY ELSE IS AROUND!

WHAT ABOUT DAD?
DAD?
SURE, ISN'T HE ALWAYS BUGGING YOU TO PLAY CATCH?
HE'D PROBABLY LOVE IT IF YOU ASKED HIM FOR A CHANGE!
HMM...

YOU'RE RIGHT, ELLEN! I'LL GIVE HIM ONE OF THOSE FATHER-SON MOMENTS AND TOTALLY MAKE HIS DAY!

DAD! HEY, DAD! WANNA HUCK A BALL AROUND?

I'M TRYING TO DO MY TAXES!

WANNA PLAY CATCH?
Peirce

NATE, YOU NEVER HANDED IN THE HOMEWORK ON THE MISSOURI COMPROMISE.
WHAT?
MRS. GODFREY

BUT I **DID** THAT HOMEWORK! I DEFINITELY REMEMBER DOING IT!
WELL, **I** NEVER GOT IT.

CHECK YOUR DESK.

STAND BACK, EVERY-BODY!
I'M GOIN' IN.
Peirce

MRS. GODFREY, I FOUND MY HOME-WORK IN MY DESK! I **TOLD** YOU I'D DONE IT!

WHOOPS, WAIT A SEC. THERE'S SOME-THING STUCK TO IT.
PIK PIK
MRS. GODFR

NIBBLE NIBBLE MUNCH MUNCH CRUNCH
MRS. GODFREY

IT'S EITHER TOMATO SAUCE OR SOME KIND OF PUDDING.
OOLP!
MRS. GODFREY
Peirce

NATE, THIS DESK IS AN ABSOLUTE DIS-GRACE! TAKE THIS JUNK TO YOUR LOCKER!
OKAY.

FOOMM!
Peirce

DONE.

NATE, THROW THIS GARBAGE AWAY.
GARBAGE? THERE'S LOTS OF GOOD STUFF IN HERE!

WELL, I SAY IT'S GARBAGE!
...AND I SAY IT HAS VALUE!

SO IF I GRAB SOMETHING AT RANDOM FROM THIS MESS, YOU CLAIM IT WILL SOMEHOW BE WORTH SOMETHING?
ABSOLUTELY!
ZWIP!

"A PRIEST, A RABBI, AND A DUCK WALK INTO A BAR..."
OH! THAT ONE'S PRICELESS!
Peirce

MY LOCKER MAY **LOOK** MESSY, MRS. GODFREY, BUT I ACT-UALLY HAVE A VERY ORGANIZED **FILING SYSTEM!**

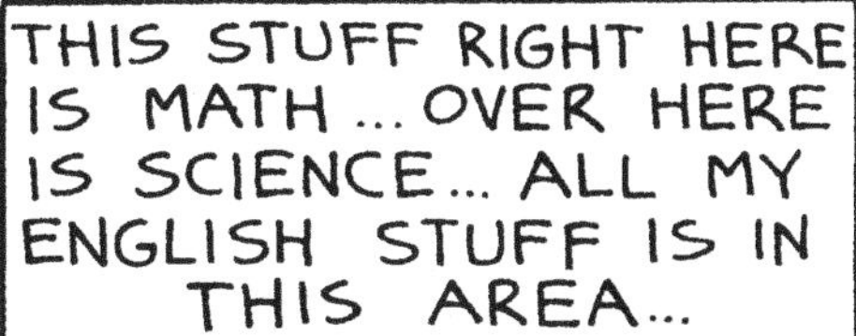
THIS STUFF RIGHT HERE IS MATH ... OVER HERE IS SCIENCE ... ALL MY ENGLISH STUFF IS IN THIS AREA ...

AND WHAT ABOUT **THIS** AREA?
UH... WAIT!...
RUSTLE RUSTLE

"MRS. GODFREY IS SO FAT, HER THIGHS HAVE LICENSE PLATES."
THAT'S PERSONAL! THAT'S **PERSONAL!**
Peirce

NATE, I'VE HEARD ENOUGH NONSENSE ABOUT YOUR LOCKER BEING SOME SORT OF PERSONAL **TREASURE TROVE**!

IT'S **TRASH**, PURE AND SIMPLE! AND I WANT IT CLEANED UP IN THE NEXT **TEN MINUTES**!!
Peirce

NOT **TWELVE** MIN-UTES! NOT **ELEVEN** MINUTES! I EXPECT YOU... YOU...

NATE?
A MESSY LOCKER DOES HAVE ITS ADVAN-TAGES.

CHESTER: PITCHING...
FRANCIS: CATCHING...
TEDDY: CENTER FIELD...
NATE: RIGHT FIELD...

AGAIN?
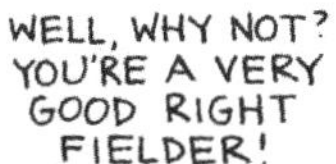
WELL, WHY NOT? YOU'RE A VERY GOOD RIGHT FIELDER!

YEAH, BUT...

NOTHING EVER HAPPENS OUT THERE!

THAT'S JUST THE WAY BASEBALL IS, NATE. SOMETIMES THEY HIT IT TO YOU, AND SOMETIMES THEY DON'T!
YEAH, I KNOW...

...BUT IT'S JUST SO BORING STANDING AROUND FOR NINE INNINGS!

JUST GET OUT THERE, NATE. I'M SURE YOU'LL FIND SOME WAY TO KEEP YOURSELF AMUSED.

Peirce

MRS. GODFREY SAYS THAT IF I DON'T START KEEPING MY DESK AND LOCKER CLEAN, IT'LL AFFECT MY **GRADE**!

BETTER NEATEN UP, DUDE.
I **CAN'T**! I'VE TRIED, BUT I **CAN'T**!

I'M JUST A MESSY PERSON! I WAS **BORN** MESSY!
WELL, TECHNIC-ALLY, I THINK **EVERY**-ONE'S BORN MESSY.

YEAH, REMEMBER THAT MOVIE WE SAW IN HEALTH CLASS?
CAN WE TALK ABOUT SOME-THING ELSE?
Peirce

SIGH...
HEY, MAYBE WE CAN HYPNO-TIZE YOU INTO BE-COMING NEATER!

IT WORKED BEFORE, REMEMBER? FRANCIS AND I HYPNOTIZED YOU TO FIND OUT WHY YOU'RE AFRAID OF CATS!

YOU'RE AFRAID OF CATS?

NATE'S AFRAID OF CATS!
THANKS SO MUCH.
OOPS.
Peirce

READY TO GET HYPNO-TIZED?
I DON'T THINK THIS IS GOING TO WORK, FRANCIS.

YOU HAVE TO BE SUGGESTIBLE TO GET HYPNOTIZED! THAT'S NOT ME! MY WILL IS TOO STRONG! MY MIND IS TOO SHARP!

SNAP!

SHARP AS A SACK OF SAND.
ZZZZZZZZZZZ
I DO THAT SAME TRICK WITH MY GERBIL!
Peirce

WHAT'S UP?
WE'RE HYPNOTIZING NATE!

HYPNO-TIZING HIM?
YUP! TO MAKE HIM LESS OF A SLOB!

MRS. GODFREY GAVE HIM AN ULTIMATUM, SO WE'RE GIVING HIM A POST-HYPNOTIC SUGGESTION TO BECOME NEATER!

CAN YOU ALSO MAKE HIM LESS ANNOY-ING?
HEY!
WE'RE HYPNO-TISTS, NOT MAGICIANS.
Peirce

OK NATE... WHEN I CLAP MY HANDS, YOU'RE GOING TO WAKE UP A CHANGED PERSON... A **NEAT** PERSON... A **TIDY** PERSON.
NEAT... TIDY...

CLAP!

YOUR GLASSES ARE FILTHY.
IT WORKED!
peirce

IT WORKED! THE HYPNOSIS WORKED!
WAIT. ARE WE SURE?

DO WE REALLY KNOW HE'S BE-COME NEAT?
WELL...
TSK!

LOOK AT THIS! WHAT A DISGRACE!

IS THERE SOME SORT OF LAW AGAINST WASHING THE BLACK-BOARD?
NOW WE KNOW.
peirce

NATE! WHAT DO YOU THINK YOU'RE DOING?
YOU TOLD ME TO KEEP MYSELF AMUSED.

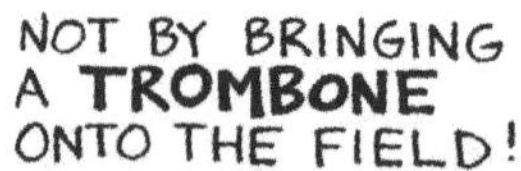
NOT BY BRINGING A TROMBONE ONTO THE FIELD!

HOW DO YOU EXPECT TO PLAY BASEBALL WHEN YOU'RE...
KRAK!

CLANG!

HOME! HOME! HE'S COMIN' HOME!

BLAST!

WUMP!

Yer OUT!
!

WHAT WERE YOU SAYING?
Peirce

MRS. GODFREY, MEET THE **NEW** NATE WRIGHT!
WE HYPNOTIZED HIM INTO BECOMING **NEAT!**

I THREW AWAY ALL THE GARBAGE IN MY LOCKER, COLOR-CODED MY FOLDERS, ALPHABETIZED MY CLASS NOTES..
TO DO

GOODNESS! WHAT A CHANGE!
YUP! I'M NOW A NEATNESS **MACHINE!** ANYTHING THAT'S **NOT** NEAT, I NOTICE IT!

WELL! I'M **VERY** IM...
...AND ON THAT NOTE, YOU'VE GOT A NASTY RUN IN YOUR PANTY HOSE.

HERE'S MY HOMEWORK, MRS. GODFREY! YOU WANT NEAT? YOU'VE GOT NEAT!

NO RIPS, NO WRINKLES, NO SMUDGES, NO STAINS! ABSOLUTELY NO MIS-TAKES OF ANY KIND!

YOU WERE SUPPOSED TO ANSWER THE TEN QUESTIONS AT THE END OF CHAPTER TWO, NOT THE TWO QUESTIONS AT THE END OF CHAPTER TEN.

OKAY, ONE TEENSY LITTLE MIS-TAKE.
TRY AGAIN.
Peirce

JENNY, M'LADY! WHAT DO YOU THINK OF THE NEW ME?
WHAT DO I CARE?
PEP RALLY!

I'VE BECOME **NEAT**, MY DEAR! NOTE THE NEW WARDROBE! NOT A WRINKLE OR CREASE ANYWHERE! I AM TOTALLY PUT TOGETHER!

SNORT! ... PUT A BOW TIE ON A PIG, IT'S STILL A PIG.

FOR SOME REASON, SHE WENT OFF ON SOME IRRELEVANT TANGENT ABOUT FARM ANIMALS.
Peirce

NOW THAT I'M NEAT, I CAN'T HELP NOTIC-ING HOW MESSY **OTHER** PEOPLE ARE!

BUT I WANT TO **HELP** PEOPLE BE NEAT LIKE **I** AM! I WANT TO SHARE MY KNOWLEDGE WITH MY FELLOW MAN!
WELL, YOU SHOULD PROBABLY KEEP THAT TO YOUR-SELF.

EXCUSE ME, DUDE, BUT YOUR PANTS ARE KIND OF FALLING DOWN. YOU MIGHT WANT TO CONSIDER A BELT.

TURNS OUT THAT MESSY PEOPLE OFTEN HAVE OTHER BEHAVIORAL ISSUES.
KEEP OUR SCHOOL CLEAN!
Peirce

I MEAN, THE GRASS IS SORT OF PATCHY... THERE'S A PUDDLE OVER THERE... AND ALL THESE ACORNS SEEM SORT OF... YOU KNOW... RANDOM.

HI, MR. WRIGHT.
FRANCIS! I'VE BEEN **HOPING** TO SEE YOU!

HERE.
WHAT'S **THIS** FOR?
!
$

WELL, DIDN'T YOU HYPNOTIZE NATE INTO BECOMING NEAT?
YEAH

CON-SIDER THAT A FINDER'S FEE.
I JUST WAXED THE FLOOR IN THE GARAGE!
Peirce

YANK!
SPUT!
SPUT!

DANG IT!
ALLOW ME, DAD! ALLOW ME!

THEY CALL ME THE "MOWER WHISPERER"!

YANK!
RRRRR

WOW! WHAT DID YOU SAY?
SORRY, DAD! TRADE SECRET!
RRRRRR

NOW IF YOU'LL EXCUSE ME, MY JOB HERE IS DONE!

NOT QUITE.
!

RRRRRRRR
Peirce

BATTER UP!
COULD YOU DUST OFF THE PLATE, PLEASE?

YUP... GOOD... UH, YOU MISSED A COUPLE SPOTS RIGHT OVER HERE...

WAIT, DON'T STOP YET! IT'S STILL DUSTY. YOU NEED TO... LOOK, WHY DON'T YOU JUST LET **ME** DO IT.

I'VE CREATED A MONSTER.
YOU WERE SUPPOSED TO MAKE HIM NEAT, NOT OBSESSIVE-COMPULSIVE.
Peirce

WHAT'S UP, MR. CLEAN?
NOW THAT I'M NEAT, I... I DON'T THINK I CAN EAT MY LUNCH.

I MEAN, LOOK AT THESE CHEEZ DOODLES! LOOK HOW THE ORANGE POWDER GETS ALL OVER EVERYTHING!... IT'S **DISGUSTING!**

BUT YOU **LOVE** CHEEZ DOODLES!
I **KNOW**, BUT THEY... I **WANT** TO EAT THEM, BUT... THEY'RE TOO **MESSY!**

ARE YOU CRYING, DUDE?
I'LL EAT THEM!
THIS IS A NIGHT-MARE.
Peirce

FRANCIS, I WANT YOU TO UN-HYPNOTIZE ME! I DON'T **LIKE** BEING NEAT!

I CAN'T **ENJOY** ANYTHING ANYMORE, BECAUSE ALL I CAN **THINK** ABOUT IS BEING **NEAT** AND **TIDY** ALL THE TIME!

BEING SO CLEAN MAKES ME FEEL... FEEL...

...DIRTY?
HOW IRONIC!
MAKE ME A SLOB AGAIN.
Peirce

NATE DOESN'T WANT TO BE NEAT ANY-MORE, SO FRANCIS IS UN-HYPNOTIZING HIM.
LET'S SEE IF IT WORKED.

SNAP!

BURRP!

THAT'S A GOOD SIGN.
HOOO! PARDON MY PRINGLES!
Peirce

HOW DO YOU FEEL, NATE?
DO YOU FEEL LIKE YOUR OLD SLOBBY SELF AGAIN?
I **THINK** SO...

HERE. EAT THIS.
OOH! BROWNIE!

NARF NARF
CHOMPF
NOMPF NARF
NOSH

HE'S BACK!
WOULD YOU LIKE A NAP-KIN?
WHAT FOR?
Peirce

HERE'S MY HOME-WORK, MRS. G!
WHA-...? THIS IS A MESS!

WHAT HAPPENED TO THE NEATNESS OF THE PAST TWO WEEKS?
THAT'S OVER! I'M BACK TO MY OLD SELF!

BUT REST ASSURED: THE PAPER MAY LOOK A BIT SLOPPY ON THE SURFACE, BUT UNDERNEATH THE QUALITY OF MY WORK IS JUST THE SAME AS EVER!

OH, GOODY.
OOP! ALMOST FORGOT! HERE'S PAGE TWO!
Peirce

WELL! HELLO, NATE!
HI, MR. EUSTIS! WOULD SPITSY LIKE TO GO FOR A WALK?

I'M SURE HE'D LOVE IT!
GREAT! C'MON, SPITSY!
wurf!

HERE, LET ME GIVE YOU A COUPLE OF BUCKS.
NOPE! NOT TODAY!

I'M WORKING ON MY "GOOD NEIGHBOR" MERIT BADGE! I'M SUPPOSED TO DO RANDOM ACTS OF KINDNESS!

THIS ISN'T A PAYING JOB! THIS IS JUST TO BE **NICE**!

YANK!

FORGET THE BADGE. I'LL TAKE THE MONEY.
Peirce

WHY DO I HAVE TO COVER **THAT** STORY? WHY CAN'T I DO THE STORY IDEA **I** PROPOSED?

MAY I HELP YOU, YOUNG MAN?
I'M HERE FOR THE SCHOOL BOARD MEETING.

I'M AFRAID TONIGHT'S MEETING ISN'T OPEN TO THE PUBLIC.
BUT I'M A REPORTER! I'M FROM THE P.S. 38 "WEEKLY BUGLE"!

WELL, YOU'LL HAVE TO BE ACCOM-PANIED BY AN ADULT.
BUT...
THE LAD IS WITH **ME**, DEAR LADY!

SCHOOL PICTURE GUY!!
IN THE FLESH, MY TRUSTY ASSISTANT!
WINKA-WINK!
!!
Peirce

FIRST TIME AT A SCHOOL BOARD MEETING, AMIGO?
YUP

WELL, LET ME GIVE YOU THE LAY OF THE LAND, MY FRIEND! I'VE ATTENDED MANY OF THESE IN MY CAPACITY AS A FREE-LANCE PHOTOGRAPHER!

THE MOST IMPORTANT THING IS TO MAKE SURE YOU'RE PROP-ERLY EQUIPPED!

WHAT'S IN THERE?
DOUGHNUTS, KID. THESE MEETINGS GIVE ME THE MUNCHIES.
Peirce

HOW COME ALL THESE PEOPLE KEEP SAYING "I MOVE THIS" AND "I SECOND THAT"?
PARLIAMENTARY PROCEDURE, MY FRIEND! IT'S A WAY OF MAINTAINING ORDER!

IT ALSO HELPS KEEP THINGS CIVIL! YOU CAN'T HAVE A SCHOOL BOARD MEETING WITH ALL THE MEMBERS SHOUTING AT EACH OTHER!

MR. CHAIRMAN, I'D LIKE TO MAKE A MOTION THAT MY DISTINGUISHED COLLEAGUE FROM DISTRICT TWO IS A PENCIL-NECKED PIN-HEAD.

SO MOVED.
I'LL SECOND THAT.
SEE? SO POLITE!

I THOUGHT YOU WERE SUPPOSED TO BE TAKING PICTURES.
MERELY WAITING FOR THE RIGHT MOMENT, KID.
MUNCH MUNCH

AT ANY SCHOOL BOARD MEETING, THERE'S A POINT WHEN TEMPERS FLARE AND DECORUM BREAKS DOWN! THAT'S WHEN YOU GET THE GOOD PHOTOS!

YOU WANT TO ELIMINATE THE DRAMA PROGRAM?? ARE YOU INSANE?

SPEAKING OF DRAMA, MARGE... CAN YOU PUT DOWN THE SCISSORS?
THIS IS JUST THE PREGAME, KID. WAIT 'TIL THEY DISCUSS THE FOOTBALL BUDGET.
Peirce

...MMPH!... I FELL ASLEEP! WHAT'S HAPPENING?
THEY'RE GOING OVER THE SCHOOL BUDGET, LINE BY LINE.

RIGHT NOW THEY'RE DISCUSSING THE "GIFTED AND TALENTED" PROGRAM, OF WHICH **I** WAS A PART BACK IN THE DAY!

YOU WERE "GIFTED AND TALENTED"?
I WAS INDEED, MON AMI!

WAIT, WAIT. **YOU** WERE...?
I SAID YES, KID. GO BACK TO SLEEP.
Peirce

FAKE FIGHT?
FAKE FIGHT!

POW!
OOF!

HYA!
ARRGH!
BOOF!
CHUCKLE!

FOOM!
HEY!

YOU CLIPPED ME FOR REAL!
OW!
SHOVE!

DON'T PUNK ME, MAN!
YOU STARTED IT, SCRUB!

LOOKS LIKE FUN, DOESN'T IT?
IF YOU SAY SO.
OW! I'M BLEEDING, YOU JERK!
JERK THIS, WUSSY BOY!
peirce

MR. GALVIN, WHAT ARE WE DOING IN CLASS TODAY?
PHOTO-SYNTHESIS.
LEMENTS

WELL... CARE TO MAKE THINGS A LITTLE MORE... INTER-ESTING?
MORE INTER...? WHAT?

ARE YOU SUGGESTING SOME SORT OF **WAGER**?

UH... I WAS SUGGESTING MAYBE A FILMSTRIP.
YEAH, PHOTO-SYNTHESIS IS REALLY BORING.
LEMENTS
Peirce

MR. GALVIN, THIS WORK-SHEET ON PHOTOSYNTHESIS REALLY ISN'T WORKING FOR ME.
IT ISN'T "WORK-ING" FOR YOU?
MR. GALVIN

WELL, LET ME EXPLAIN SOMETHING, NATE. THE WORKSHEET ISN'T "WORKING" FOR YOU BECAUSE IT'S A PIECE OF PAPER! IT'S NOT SUPPOSED TO "WORK"!

THE "WORK" PART IS WHERE YOU COME IN! YOU "WORK" ON THE "SHEET"! WHICH IS WHY IT'S CALLED A WORK-SHEET!
MR. GALVIN

THAT DIDN'T WORK.
Peirce

MR. GALVIN, THE CLASS HAS APPOINTED ME AS ITS SPOKESMAN.
SPOKES-MAN FOR WHAT?

WE WANT TO STOP STUDYING PHOTO-SYNTHESIS AND START STUDY-ING SOMETHING GOOD!
"GOOD"?

WELL, THAT'S FASCIN-ATING, NATE. SUPPOSE YOU TELL ME WHAT SUBJECT MATTER WOULD QUALIFY AS "GOOD."

WE'VE NARROWED IT DOWN TO EITHER HUMAN REPRODUCTION OR A FIELD TRIP TO "SEA WORLD."
CRIPES.
Peirce

MR. GALVIN NEEDS TO LIGHTEN UP.
HEY, **THERE'S** A NEWS FLASH.

I'M SERIOUS! HAVE YOU EVER SEEN THE MAN **LAUGH**?
LAUGH? I'VE NEVER EVEN SEEN HIM **SMILE**!

I'LL BET **I** COULD GET A CHUCKLE OUT OF HIM!
YOU? HOW?

HAVE YOU FORGOTTEN ABOUT MY LEGENDARY ARSENAL OF "KNOCK KNOCK" JOKES?
SADLY, NO.
"ARSENAL" IS RIGHT.

MR. GALVIN, I'VE GOT A JOKE FOR YOU! WHAT DID THE CAVEMAN SAY TO THE T. REX?

GIVE UP?
NATE, A CAVEMAN COULDN'T HAVE SAID ANYTHING TO A T. REX. ALL SPECIES OF DINOSAURS PERISHED AT THE END OF THE CRETACEOUS PERIOD.

COMBINE THAT WITH THE FACT THAT THE EARLIEST ANCESTORS OF HOMO SAPIENS DIDN'T APPEAR UNTIL THE PLIOCENE EPOCH, AND THE SCENARIO YOU PROPOSE...

FORTY YEARS OF TEACHING MIDDLE SCHOOL SCIENCE DOES SOMETHING TO A PERSON.
Peirce

OKAY, MR. GALVIN... **HERE'S** A JOKE I THINK YOU'LL APPREC-IATE!

WHAT DID THE THEORETICAL PHYSICIST USE TO DRINK HIS BEER?

AN EIN-STEIN!
WA HA HA HA HA HA HA HO HO HA

WHAT KIND OF A SCIENCE TEACHER DOESN'T LAUGH AT A JOKE ABOUT THEORETICAL PHYSICS?
Peirce

I'VE BEEN TRYING ALL WEEK TO GET MR. GALVIN TO LAUGH, BUT IT'S IMPOSSIBLE!

I'VE TOLD HIM EVERY JOKE I KNOW! EVERY RIDDLE!!

...BUT NOTHING!
I CAN GET HIM TO LAUGH!

YOU?? SNORT! RIGHT, GINA!
I'LL BET YOU FIVE BUCKS!

YOU'RE ON!
FOLLOW ME!

MR. GALVIN, NATE THINKS HE HAS A GOOD CHANCE TO MAKE THE HONOR ROLL THIS TERM. WHAT DO YOU THINK?

WELL, I... MMMPH!
AHEM! CHUCKLE!... HEH HEH...

WA HA HA HA HA HA HA HA HA HA

OH, THE INDIGNITY.
YOU KNOW, THAT WAS WORTH FIVE BUCKS!
Peirce

IT'S A SCHOOL RULE THAT CLUBS NEED TO HAVE A TEACHER PRESENT AT MEETINGS, AND WE FIGURED YOU PROBABLY DON'T HAVE ANYTHING ELSE GOING ON!

GUYS, I CONVINCED CHAD TO JOIN THE CARTOONING CLUB!
COOL!
HEY, CHAD.

PULL UP A CHAIR, CHAD!
UH... WHERE ARE ALL THE GIRLS?

YOU SAID THERE WERE LOTS OF GIRLS AT THESE MEETINGS.
RIGHT! GIRLS WE **DRAW!**
Peirce

MY NEWEST CHARACTER: RAMONA BOMBSHELLE!
ROWR! HEL-**LO!**

WHEN DRAWING COMICS, CHAD, COMING UP WITH THE RIGHT SOUND EFFECT IS CRUCIAL!

ALMOST ANY SITUATION CAN BE MADE FUNNY BY THE ADDITION OF A HUMOROUS SOUND EFFECT!

KLONG!

PROPS ARE ALSO KEY!
OW!
YOU'RE BOTH RIGHT!
Peirce

I NEED A SOUND EFFECT. WHAT DOES A GARBAGE DISPOSAL SOUND LIKE?
SORT OF LIKE: KRPBLKRPB!

YES! YES! THAT'S PERFECT!

HOW DO YOU SPELL THAT?
JUST LIKE IT SOUNDS.
Peirce

WHEN DRAWING A COMIC STRIP, CHAD, YOU DON'T ALWAYS HAVE TO WAIT UNTIL THE FINAL PANEL TO DELIVER THE PUNCH LINE!

SOMETIMES YOU CAN PUT THE JOKE IN THE **NEXT-TO-LAST** PANEL! THEN THE **LAST** PANEL CAN BE JUST, YOU KNOW, A REACTION SHOT!

WOO
WOO
WOO
WOO
WOO
BOING!
BOING!

NOW, WHERE WAS I?
Peirce

MR. ROSA, ARE WE ALLOWED TO DRAW COMICS ABOUT TEACHERS?
PROVIDED THEY'RE NOT IN-APPROPRIATE.
OONING CLUB

"INAPPROPRIATE"?
YOU KNOW... MEAN-SPIRITED.

"MEAN-SPIRITED"?
NEEDLESSLY CRUEL.

DEFINE "NEEDLESSLY."
TELL YOU WHAT, SON, WHY DON'T YOU JUST FOCUS ON SUPERHEROES FOR NOW.
CLUB
Peirce

TIME, PEOPLE! HAND 'EM IN!
WRITE
WRITE
WRITE
WRITE
WRITE
WRITE
WRITE

THANK YOU, NATE.
GRUMBLE..

HOW'D YOU DO?
I THOUGHT IT WAS EASY! REALLY EASY!
ME TOO!

WHAT'D YOU THINK, NATE?
HM?

OH!... UH... YEAH!... IT WAS EASY! SO EASY!

HEH! I SURE HOPE THE FINAL IS THAT EASY!

THAT WAS THE FINAL.

COMIN' THROUGH.

I'M HERE FOR DETENTION, MRS. CZERWICKI.
AGAIN? NATE, WHY?

WELL... I MISSED YOU.
YOU... YOU MISSED ME?
!
COUNT TO TEN!

WHY, NATE, HOW VERY SWEET! I DON'T KNOW WHAT TO...
YEAH, I HUCKED A CUPCAKE AT YOU WHILE YOU WERE ON LUNCH DUTY...

... AND INSTEAD I HIT THAT SNITCH MIRANDA KILGORE.
GO SIT DOWN, SON.
peirce

"WHILE EXCAVATING THE TOMB OF HAKHOTAN, SHAPELY SCIENTIST MAURA ALBRIGHT FINDS HERSELF EN- CHANTED BY THE RUGGED EGYPTOLOGIST ADAM CASSEL, BEHIND WHOSE ICY BLUE EYES BURNS A FIRE HOTTER THAN THE DESERT SUN."

HOW COME YOU ALWAYS READ THOSE ROMANCE NOVELS, MRS. CZERWICKI?
OH, I KNOW THEY'RE TRASHY...

...BUT I GUESS THEY'RE A TYPE OF ESCAPISM.
ESCAPISM?

ESCAPISM FROM WHAT?

TWO HOURS LATER...
...AND THEN ON OUR ANNIVERSARY, HE TOOK ME TO A HOCKEY GAME!
YIKES.
peirce

FIRST TIME, KID?
YES. ARE THEY GOING TO CALL MY PARENTS?

YUP. THEY ALWAYS CALL YOUR PARENTS WHEN YOU GET DETENTION.
OHHH... THEY'RE GOING TO BE SO MAD.

KID, RELAX. MY DAD WAS UPSET THE FIRST COUPLE TIMES, BUT AFTER A FEW DOZEN, HE GOT USED TO IT.

A FEW DOZEN?
WHEN I HIT TRIPLE DIGITS, HE JUST BECAME NUMB.
Peirce

THIS IS BORING.
THAT'S THE WHOLE POINT.

DETENTION IS MEANT TO BREAK OUR SPIRIT! BY KEEPING US **TRAPPED** IN HERE, THEY'RE TRYING TO **BORE** US INTO BE-COMING **OBEDIENT!** IT'S **WRONG!**

WE'VE GOT TO **RESIST** THEM BY **CONTINU-ING** THE BEHAVIOR THAT LANDED US HERE IN THE **FIRST** PLACE!

SO... THE WAY TO FIGHT AGAINST DETENTION IS TO KEEP **GETTING** DETENTION?
YOU'RE CATCHING ON, KID. SAME TIME TOMORROW.
Peirce

YOU MAY BE HAPPY GETTING DETENTION EVERY DAY, BUT NOT ME!

ONCE IS ENOUGH! I'VE LEARNED MY LESSON! I'M NEVER GOING TO GET DE-TENTION AGAIN!

I'M GOING TO TURN MY LIFE AROUND! I'M GOING TO BE THE TYPE OF STUDENT THIS SCHOOL CAN BE PROUD OF!

WHAT A LOSER.
Peirce

SIR? I HAVE A NOTE FOR YOU FROM NATE WRIGHT.
FROM NATE WRIGHT?
ITALY
MR. NICHOLS

HE DROPPED IT OFF ON HIS WAY TO CLASS.
ALL RIGHT THEN. THANK YOU, MRS. SHIPULSKI.
RIP

Dear Principal Nichols,
Hi there, big guy. I hope your morning is going OK so far.

I just want to take a moment to let you know what a great principal you are. You do an awesome job as the leader of our school.

You inspire confidence and make us feel safe. And speaking of safety, I couldn't help noticing we haven't had a fire drill recently.

So, could we have a fire drill this morning? And could it happen at precisely 9:30?
MR. NICHOLS

Thanks!
Sincerely,
Nate Wright
CLUNK!

YOU HAVE FORTY MINUTES TO COMPLETE THIS TEST. BEGIN.
I SHOULD HAVE INCLUDED A BRIBE.
Peirce

PRINCIPAL NICHOLS! WHAT ARE YOU DOING OUT HERE?
JUST GREETING STUDENTS, THAT'S ALL!
? ?

IT'S SUCH A BEAUTIFUL DAY, I SIMPLY **HAD** TO BE OUTSIDE, SAYING "GOOD MORNING"!

I'M THE LEADER OF THIS SCHOOL, AND IT'S MY RESPONSIBILITY TO MAKE YOU KIDS FEEL **WELCOME**!

PLUS, MY OFFICE IS BEING PAINTED.
? ?
Peirce

RRRRINNNGG!
GOOD GRAVY! THAT'S THE FIRST PERIOD BELL, AND I'VE GOT **NOTHING** PREPARED!

MR. ROSA! SINCE THE WEATHER'S SO NICE, CAN WE HAVE CLASS OUTSIDE?

OUTSI...?... YES!... **YES!!** OUTSIDE!! LANDSCAPE DRAWING, EVERYBODY! GRAB YOUR SKETCHBOOKS!
YAAAAYY

AH, LESSON PLAN-NING.
PEIRCE

MRS. GODFREY, SINCE THE WEATHER IS SO NICE, CAN WE HAVE CLASS OUTSIDE? PLEEEZ?
NO.

BUT MR. ROSA LET US HAVE **ART** OUTSIDE, AND IT WAS **AWESOME**!

I'M NOT MR. ROSA.

SHE'S NOT MR. ROSA.
NEWS FLASH.
Peirce

MR. GALVIN, CAN WE HAVE CLASS OUT-SIDE? IT COULD BE **VERY** EDU-CATIONAL!

LET'S GET OUT IN THE FIELD LIKE REAL SCIENTISTS! WE'LL STUDY ECO-SYSTEMS! WE'LL DO RESEARCH!

YOU HAVE A FRISBEE HIDDEN IN YOUR NOTE-BOOK.

THAT'S FOR COLLECT-ING SOIL SAMPLES.
THERE'S A HACKY SACK IN YOUR POCKET.
Peirce

MS. CLARKE, CAN WE HAVE CLASS OUTSIDE?
OUT-SIDE?

MR. ROSA SAID YES. MRS. GODFREY AND MR. GALVIN SAID NO.

ARE YOU GOING TO ALLY YOUR-SELF WITH ROSA, OR WITH GODFREY AND GALVIN?

WELL PLAYED.
I UNDER-STAND FACULTY DYNAMICS.
Peirce

MR. STAPLES, IT'S SUCH A NICE DAY THAT WE'VE BEEN ASKING TEACHERS TO LET US HAVE CLASS OUTSIDE.

TWO TEACHERS HAVE SAID **YES**, TWO HAVE SAID **NO**. WE HAVE A **TIE**, AND ONLY **YOU** CAN BREAK IT!

THE CLOCK IS TICKING, MR. STAPLES.
IT'S HERO TIME.

SCORE!
I HAPPEN TO KNOW THE MAN PLAYED DIVISION 3 BASKETBALL!
Peirce

CHECK THIS OUT.

HEY NATE: WHO WAS THE MVP OF SUPER BOWL XV?
JIM PLUNKETT.

WHAT TEACHER DOES LINUS HAVE A CRUSH ON IN "PEANUTS"?
MISS OTHMAR.

WHAT'S JACKIE CHAN'S REAL NAME?
CHAN KONG-SANG.

WHAT YEAR WAS ZZ TOP INDUCTED INTO THE ROCK AND ROLL HALL OF FAME?
2004.

WHO DIRECTED "NACHO LIBRE"?
JARED HESS.

WHAT'S TWELVE TIMES SEVEN?

UHHH...

WAIT. LET ME THINK.
FASCINATING.
IT ALSO WORKS WITH STATE CAPITALS.
Peirce

LAST DAY OF SCHOOL TOMORROW! PRANK DAY!
OOH, YEAH! PRANK DAY!

SO LONG, PRINCIPAL NICHOLS! SEE YOOOOUU....

......TOMORROW!
BWA HA HA HA HA HAAAAA!

THAT'S FUN!
I LOVE IT WHEN YOU CAN SMELL THEIR FEAR!
Peirce

IT'S PRANK DAY, NATE! WHAT ARE YOU GONNA DO?
YEAH, NATE! WHAT ARE YOU GONNA DO?

LADS, SOMETIMES IT'S NOT WHAT YOU'RE **GOING** TO DO...

GUYS! COME SEE! SOMEBODY FILLED THE FACULTY PARKING LOT WITH CHOCOLATE PUDDING!

... IT'S WHAT YOU'VE ALREADY DONE.

ALL RIGHT, PEOPLE, SETTLE DOWN! THERE WILL BE NO "PRANK DAY" SHENANIGANS IN **THIS** ROOM!

WE STILL HAVE ONE FINAL CLASS TO GET THROUGH, AND...
DELIVERY.

WHAT?
THE "THIGHMASTER" YOU ORDERED, MA'AM.

HA HA HA HA
HA
CRIPES.
HI, KIDS.
HA HA
HA
HA HA
Peirce

SNICKER! I LOVE PRANK DAY! I JUST THREW A WATER BALLOON INTO THE COPIER ROOM!
...AND I SWITCHED THE SIGNS ON THE BOYS AND GIRLS LOCKER ROOMS!

I TOOK A RECORDING OF PRINCIPAL NICHOLS SINGING KARAOKE AND PROGRAMMED IT TO PLAY OVER THE INTER-COM IN EXACTLY...

...3...2...1...

SOME PEOPLE CALL ME THE SPACE COWBOY....
KILLER!
!
I'M A PRO.
peirce

CHUCKLE! SOMEBODY PUT FAKE POOP ON MR. GALVIN'S DESK!
WAS IT **YOU**, NATE?

SNORT! PLEASE.

ATTENTION, TEACHERS AND STUDENTS: THE MUSIC ROOM IS TEMPORARILY OFF-LIMITS...

...BECAUSE **SOME-BODY** PUT A **LLAMA** IN IT!!
THAT WAS ME.
Peirce

SUMMER VACATION STARTS IN TWENTY SECONDS!
WHAT SHOULD WE DO FIRST?
I'M GOING ON A DIET!

A DIET?
YUP! I'M ABOUT TO LOSE... OH, I'D SAY AROUND FIFTEEN POUNDS!

WUMP!
KEEP OUR SCHOO CLEA

RRRRIINNGG!!
Peirce

AHH, SUMMER!

NO SCHOOL TO THINK ABOUT! NO TEACHERS TO BOSS US AROUND! WE'RE FREE!

WE CAN DO ANYTHING WE WANT! THE POSSIBILITIES ARE ENDLESS! IT'S A BIG WORLD OUT THERE!

! MR. GALVIN!
YOU'RE JAYWALKING, BOYS. USE THE CROSS-WALK.

FIND SOMEWHERE ELSE TO PLAY FRISBEE, BOYS. YOU MIGHT HIT SOMEONE.
PRINCIPAL NICHOLS!

HOW'S THAT OFF-SEASON CONDITIONING PROGRAM GOING, LADIES?
COACH JOHN!

IF YOU WANT TO HAVE A PRAYER OF COMPLETING THE SUMMER READING LIST, I SUGGEST YOU HEAD FOR THE LIBRARY.
!
!

IT MIGHT BE A BIG WORLD, BUT IT'S A SMALL, SMALL TOWN.
I CAN'T WAIT TO GO OFF TO COLLEGE.
Peirce

AWAKE ALREADY? DURING SUMMER VACATION?
YUP. I'M "SCHOOL-LAGGED."

MY BODY'S STILL ON A SCHOOL SCHEDULE, SO I WOKE UP AT 6:45, JUST LIKE A REGULAR SCHOOL DAY!

...BUT THERE IS NO SCHOOL, SO I'M GOING BACK TO BED! HAVE FUN AT WORK, DAD!

AND CAN YOU NOT SING IN THE SHOWER? THAT GIVES ME NIGHT-MARES.
Peirce

READY TO HIT THE BEACH?
NOT YET. WAIT A SEC.

WHAT'S THE HOLD-UP?
JUST LISTEN.

RRRRRIIINNNNNGGG!!

IS THERE ANY SOUND SWEETER THAN A SCHOOL BELL IN SUMMER?
Peirce

I THINK NOT.

SAME HERE.

AHHHHH, VACATION!
Peirce

WHAT TIME IS IT?
11:28

OOP! WE'D BETTER GET A MOVE ON! WE'VE GOT MATH IN TWO MINUTES!

WA HA HA HA HA HA HA HA HA HA HA HA

MAYBE THAT'LL GET OLD BY AUGUST, BUT FOR NOW IT'S **HILARIOUS!**
SUMMER MAKES US GIDDY!

IT'S 12:30! IF WE WERE IN SCHOOL RIGHT NOW, WE'D BE SITTING IN MRS. GODFREY'S CLASS LISTENING TO HER YAMMERING ABOUT... ABOUT...

...HEY, WHAT'S THE NAME OF THAT GUY SHE TOLD US ABOUT LAST WEEK?
WHO **CARES**? WHY EVEN **THINK** ABOUT IT?

YEAH, BUT NOW THAT I CAN'T THINK OF IT, IT'S DRIVING ME CRAZY.
QUIT THINKING ABOUT IT! IT'S **SUMMER**! DON'T **RUIN** IT!

MA'AM? WHO WAS THE GUY WHO RAN FOR PRESIDENT AGAINST ABE LINCOLN AND THEN ENDED UP AS THE SECRETARY OF....
YOU'RE RUIN-ING IT!!
Peirce

FRANCIS?... DUDE, HOW COME YOU'RE NOT AT THE BEACH? IT'S AWESOME! THE WATER IS **PERFECT!**

WHAT?... WELL, TELL YOUR MOM YOU'LL DO IT **LATER!** YOU CAN'T WASTE A PRIMO BEACH DAY LIKE THIS!

YEAH, THE BODY-SURFING IS **INCRED-IBLE!** I'VE NEVER SEEN THE WAVES SO...

HELLO?
Peirce

WHAT'S WITH THE STICK?
JUST MAKING A POINT, TEDDY.

I KEEP TELLING COACH THAT NOTHING EVER HAPPENS OUT HERE IN RIGHT FIELD!

TO PROVE MY POINT, I'M MARKING THIS SPOT!

...AND I'LL BET I WON'T HAVE TO MOVE FROM THIS SPOT FOR THE WHOLE GAME!

CRACK!

WELL! LOOKS LIKE I WILL HAVE TO MOVE!

OOP! IT'S NOT CARRYING LIKE I THOUGHT IT WOULD!

ARRGH! NOW THE WIND'S TAKING IT!

THE SUN'S IN MY EYES! WHERE IS IT?

THERE IT IS!

NAB!

Peirce

DAD! CAN I MEET FRANCIS AT THE BEACH?

WE'VE GOT OTHER PLANS, NATE. REMEMBER?
OH...RIGHT.

SORRY, DUDE. I CAN'T GO TO THE BEACH.

...ALTHOUGH I'LL BE SPENDING MOST OF THE DAY AROUND SAND AND WATER.
FORE!
Peirce

I'M GOING TO TRY WHAT I READ IN MY GOLF MAGAZINE!

GRIP IT!... RIP IT!...

POW!

...AND DIP IT.
I THINK IT'S MORE OVER THAT WAY.

DID YOU FIND MY BALL?
I'M NOT SURE. WHAT BALL WERE YOU PLAYING?

WHAT DID YOU FIND?
WHAT WERE YOU PLAYING?
WHAT DID YOU FIND?

TOP-FLITE 4.
THAT'S MY BALL!

TOUGH SHOT HERE, DAD. YOU'VE GOT 183 YARDS TO THE FRONT OF A SLOPING GREEN, AND YOUR BALL'S ON A DOWNHILL LIE.

IF YOU HIT A LOW FADE, YOU CAN AVOID THAT TREE, LAND IT ON THE FRINGE, AND LET IT RUN UP TO THE PIN.
RIGHT!

THIS IS FOR TRIPLE BOGEY.

THAT LAST COMMENT PUT A DENT IN MY "POSITIVE VISUALIZATION" ROUTINE.
WAIT, MY BAD. QUAD**RUPLE** BOGEY
Peirce

HERE COMES THE GIRL WITH THE SNACK CART! CAN WE GET A COUPLE SODAS, DAD?
OKAY. JUST LET ME HIT THIS SHOT.

WAK!

CLONG!

GOOD THING SHE WAS WEARING THAT BIKE HELMET.
I REALLY WASN'T THIRSTY ANYWAY.
Peirce

I LOVE GOLF, BUT I'VE NEVER REALLY PLAYED A ROUND THAT **MEANS** ANYTHING!

I'D LOVE TO KNOW WHAT IT WOULD FEEL LIKE TO BE A PRO! TO PLAY FOR **HIGH STAKES**!

I'D LOVE TO FIND OUT HOW I'D REACT UNDER **PRESSURE**!
YOU WANT PRESSURE?

YOU'RE DOWN TO YOUR LAST BALL, AND WE'RE ONLY ON THE TWELFTH HOLE.
YIKES.
PEIRCE

IT WAS FILLED WITH ALL SORTS OF WISE SAY-INGS LIKE "THE EARLY BIRD GETS THE WORM" AND "A PENNY SAVED IS A PENNY EARNED"!

"POOR NATE'S ALMANAC" IS THE SAME THING, ONLY **BETTER!** YOU WON'T BELIEVE ALL THE WIS-DOM IN HERE!

There's a sucker born every minute.

THERE! THAT'S DONE!
WHAT'S DONE?
BOOP!

I JUST REGISTERED FOR MY FIRST ROAD RACE! A 10K!
COOL. CONGRATULATIONS, DAD.

CHUCKLE!... WELL, DON'T CONGRATULATE ME **NOW!** CONGRATULATE ME WHEN I **FINISH** THE **RACE!**
WHAT IF YOU DON'T FINISH?

WHAT A CHEERY THOUGHT.
EXACTLY. ON RACE DAY I DON'T WANT TO BE, LIKE: "DAD! NICE **HEART ATTACK!**"

I DON'T WANT TO RAIN ON YOUR PARADE, DAD, BUT DO YOU REALLY THINK YOU CAN RUN A 10K?
WHY NOT?

IT'S OVER SIX MILES!
SO? LOOK, I ALREADY DO A DAILY LAP AROUND THE BLOCK!

TO TRAIN FOR THE RACE, ALL I NEED TO DO IS INCREASE THAT BY A LAP OR TWO!
...OR TWENTY-FOUR.

TWENTY-FOUR?
AND SPEAKING OF TRAINING... MIGHT BE A GOOD IDEA TO LOSE THE DOUGHNUT.
Peirce

DAD, IF YOU'RE GONNA RUN A 10K, YOU SHOULD LET ME BE YOUR TRAINER.
WHY'S THAT?

BECAUSE I KNOW WHAT I'M DOING! REMEMBER, I HAD TO RUN A 5-MILER TO GET MY PHYSICAL FITNESS MERIT BADGE!

THERE'S STUFF YOU NEED TO KNOW, DAD! THERE ARE "DOS" AND "DON'TS" IN THE WORLD OF RUNNING!

THE SOCKS, FOR INSTANCE, ARE A "DON'T."
THEY ARE?
Peirce

GOING FOR A TRAINING RUN, DAD? YOU NEED TO STRETCH FIRST.
BUT I STRETCHED ALREADY!

ALL YOU DID WAS LEAN AGAINST A WALL FOR FIVE SECONDS! BEND OVER AND TOUCH YOUR TOES FOR A TEN-COUNT!
OKAY.

RRIIIP!

WAS THAT MY HAMSTRING?
JUST A WARD-ROBE MALFUNCTION, DAD. GO CHANGE YOUR SHORTS.
Peirce

WHAT'S GOING ON?
I'M HELPING MY DAD TRAIN FOR A 10K, FRANCIS.

I ALREADY HAD HIM RUN SOME HILLS, AND NOW HE'S DOING A FEW LAPS AROUND THE BLOCK AT A MODERATE PACE.

IS HE SUPPOSED TO BE CHASING AFTER THAT ICE CREAM TRUCK?
DAD! NO DE-TOURS!
PEIRCE

HAS YOUR DAD EVER RUN A 10K BEFORE?
NOPE. FIRST TIME.

AND WHEN'S THE RACE?
IN FOUR WEEKS.

SHOULD BE AN ENTER-TAINING MONTH!
DAD! GET UP!
Peirce

AARRGH!

WHAT HAPPENED? DID I JERK MY HEAD UP?
NOPE

DID I ROLL MY WRISTS?
NOPE

WAS I PAST HORIZONTAL ON MY BACKSWING?
NO
DID MY FRONT HIP FLY OPEN?
NO

DID I TURN MY SHOULDERS TOO EARLY?
NOPE

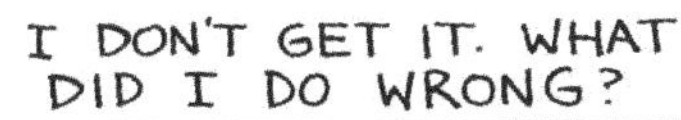
I DON'T GET IT. WHAT DID I DO WRONG?

WHAT DID I DO WRONG?

YOU HIT YOUR BALL INTO THE WOODS.

WRONG ANSWER.
KEEP LOOKING.

MAN, I'M SO BROKE.
ME TOO.
YOU KNOW WHAT WE SHOULD DO? GO TO A **YARD SALE**!

WE TAKE THE LITTLE BIT OF **CASH** WE HAVE, SEE, AND WE BUY SOMETHING! SOMETHING THAT **LOOKS** LIKE A WORTHLESS PIECE OF **JUNK**!

...BUT THEN WE TAKE IT ON "ANTIQUES ROADSHOW" AND FIND OUT IT'S ACTUALLY WORTH A **FORTUNE**!

AND THEN WE'LL HAVE ENOUGH MONEY TO GO SEE "EVAN ALMIGHTY"?
RIGHT! WITH UN-LIMITED "JUNIOR MINTS"!

WHAT ARE YOU DOING?
CHECKING OUT THE YARD SALE LISTINGS!

THERE'S ONE ONLY FOUR BLOCKS FROM HERE THAT SOUNDS LIKE THE IDEAL PLACE TO PICK UP SOME UNDERVALUED **TREASURES!**

"BABY CLOTHES, LAWN FURNITURE, PICTURE FRAMES, NEARLY NEW SNOW TIRES, SHEET MUSIC, USED POWER TOOLS, AND MUCH MORE."

A VERITABLE GOLD MINE.
"AND MUCH MORE"! THAT'S, LIKE, **CODE** FOR "**KA-CHING!**"
Peirce

OKAY, LADS, START LOOKING FOR STUFF WE CAN BUY CHEAP, THEN RESELL FOR A HUGE PROFIT!
YARD SALE

OH HO! A MAGIC EIGHT BALL!
A MAGIC EIGHT BALL? HOW IS THAT GONNA MAKE US A PROFIT?

MAGIC EIGHT BALL!... WILL FRANCIS, TEDDY AND I BUY SOMETHING AT THIS YARD SALE THAT'S WORTH WAY MORE THAN WE PAY FOR IT?
SHUCKA SHUCKA SHUCKA

"IT IS CERTAIN." YES!
I'M SO GLAD WE'RE APPROACHING THIS SCIENTIFICALLY.
Peirce

GUYS, HELP ME PEEK BEHIND THE BACK OF THIS PAINTING!
WHAT FOR?

HAVEN'T YOU HEARD ABOUT THAT GUY WHO BOUGHT AN OLD PAINTING AT A YARD SALE?

LATER, WHEN HE TOOK OFF THE BACK-ING, HE FOUND A COPY OF THE **DECLARATION OF INDEPENDENCE!**

DUDE, THIS IS A VELVET SILKSCREEN OF DOGS PLAYING POKER.
EXACTLY! WHERE BETTER TO HIDE VALUABLES? BEHIND A **CLASSIC!**

AHEM!... UH... HOW MUCH FOR THIS JUNKY OL' PICTURE?
HM?...TEN CENTS.

SOLD! HA! MY GOOD MAN, YOU MAY HAVE JUST MADE ME RICH!

THIS PICTURE YOU JUST SOLD ME FOR A DIME LOOKS TO BE AN AUTHENTIC PHOTOGRAPH OF A YOUNG ABE LINCOLN!

KID, THAT'S A POSTCARD OF KEANU REEVES THAT MY DAUGHTER DREW A BEARD ON WITH A "SHARPIE."
IT IS?
SMOOTH MOVE, EX-LAX.

MISTER, THIS YARD SALE ISN'T EX-ACTLY A TREASURE TROVE.

THERE'S NOTHING HERE I COULD TAKE TO "ANTIQUES ROADSHOW" AND FIND OUT IT'S WORTH A LOT OF MONEY! THERE'S NOTHING HERE OF VALUE!

IT'S ALMOST LIKE... YOU'RE JUST TRYING TO SELL STUFF YOU HAVE NO USE FOR ANYMORE!

NO OFFENSE.
NONE TAKEN. YOU GONNA BUY THAT?
Peirce

THREE MORE, AND YOU'LL BREAK YOUR ALL-TIME RECORD!
NO PROB-LEM!

SWISH!

TWO MORE! THAT'S PRESSURE SHOOTING!
"PRESSURE"? WHAT IS THIS "PRESSURE" YOU SPEAK OF?

SWISH!
I DON'T EVEN KNOW THE **MEANING** OF PRESSURE!
HELLO, BOYS.
MRS. GODFREY!
ULP!

I'M ON MY WAY OVER TO A READING AT THAT NEW BOOKSTORE!
HM.
UH HUH

OH, BUT I DIDN'T MEAN TO IN-TERRUPT YOU! KEEP SHOOT-ING, NATE!
UH... OKAY.

CLANG!

TSK! SO CLOSE!

NOW DO YOU KNOW THE MEAN-ING OF PRESSURE?
OH, HOW I HATE HER.
Peirce

YOU GUYS ARE IN TROUBLE TODAY! WE'VE GOT OUR **ACE** PITCHING!
OH, REALLY? THAT'S NICE.

YUP, HE'S ALMOST SIX FEET TALL, AND HE CAN **BRING** IT!
HM. YEAH, HE'S PRETTY BIG.

OUR PITCHER'S OVER THERE.

WHA...? WHA...? WHA...?
DO YOU LIKE THE FULL BEARD? SEE, I THINK HE LOOKED BETTER WITH JUST A MUSTACHE.
Peirce

CHESTER SEEMED SLUGGISH WARMING UP. HIS FASTBALL WAS SLOWER THAN USUAL.
I'LL FIX THAT.

CHESTER PITCHES BEST WHEN HE PITCHES **ANGRY**! SO ALL WE HAVE TO DO IS MAKE HIM **MAD**!

HOW DO WE...
YO, CHESTER! FRANCIS JUST CALLED YOU "SLOW"!

WHAT?!
THERE YOU GO! PROBLEM SOLVED!
Peirce

THESE GUYS ARE PRETTY COCKY, CHESTER! HOW ABOUT SHUTTING THEM UP BY PITCHING A NO-HITTER?

CHESTER?
I'M TRYING TO DO MY PRE-GAME ROUTINE.

I'M TRYING TO GO TO MY HAPPY PLACE. I DON'T LIKE PEOPLE BOTHERING ME WHEN I'M IN MY HAPPY PLACE.

HEAR THAT, FELLAS? BACK OFF!
GET OUT OF MY HAPPY PLACE OR I'LL RIP YOUR ARM OFF.
Peirce

ATTABOY, CHESTER! NICE PITCHING!
IT'S GOOD THAT YOU CAUGHT THAT FLY BALL.

IF YOU HADN'T CAUGHT THAT FLY BALL, YOU WOULD HAVE MADE ME MAD.

IF YOU MISS ANY FLY BALLS DURING THE REST OF THE GAME, YOU'RE GOING TO MAKE ME MAD.

FOR THE FIRST TIME IN MY LIFE, I'M PRAYING FOR A RAIN OUT.

NICE HIT.
HM? OH... THANKS.
DUST DUST

I'M SURPRISED YOU HIT IT TO THE OPPO-SITE FIELD. OUR SCOUTING REPORT SAID YOU'RE A DEAD PULL HITTER.
SCOUTING REPORT?

YOU GUYS HAVE A SCOUTING REPORT ON ME?
YUP.

HEY COACH! I'VE BEEN SCOUTED!
GOOD, NATE. STAY ON THE BASE.

I STILL CAN'T BELIEVE THE OTHER TEAM HAD A **SCOUTING REPORT** ON ME!
SO YOU KEEP SAYING.

Y'KNOW, IT WOULDN'T SURPRISE ME IF SOME **PRO** SCOUTS HAVE THEIR EYES ON ME!
PRO SCOUTS? YOU'RE **ELEVEN YEARS OLD!**

SO? TAKE A LOOK AT THAT GUY UP THERE! HAVE YOU NOTICED HE'S AT ALL OUR GAMES? HAVE YOU SEEN THE WAY HE'S ALWAYS WRITING ON THAT NOTEPAD?

DUDE, THAT'S MY UNCLE PEDRO.
OH.
AND I THINK HE'S DOING AN "ACROSTIC."

FRANCIS! DO YOU BELIEVE IN OMENS?
I GUESS SO.

WELL, IF I MAKE THIS SHOT, IT'S AN OMEN THAT I'M GOING TO BE RICH!

IF I MAKE IT WITHOUT HITTING THE BACKBOARD, IT MEANS I'M GOING TO BE FAMOUS!

...AND IF I MAKE IT WITHOUT HITTING THE BACKBOARD **OR** THE RIM, IT MEANS I'M GOING TO MARRY A SUPER-MODEL!

FLING!

CLANG!

CRASH!
MYOWR!
Screeee..
THUMP!

WHAT IF YOU MISS, AND THEN THE BALL BREAKS A WINDOW, HITS A CAT, ROLLS INTO THE STREET, AND GETS RUN OVER BY A DUMP TRUCK?
THEN IT'S A PRACTICE SHOT.

WHO'S THE GUY PAINTING THE LAND-SCAPE?
RUSTY SIENNA! AMERICA'S GREATEST TV ARTIST!

WHAT'S SO GREAT ABOUT RUSTY SIENNA?
IT'S HIS WHOLE APPROACH! HIS WHOLE RELATION-SHIP WITH NATURE!

WITH NATURE?
RIGHT.

BUT HE'S PAINTING INSIDE A DARK-ENED ROOM.
IN BODY, YES. BUT IN SPIRIT, HE'S TREK-KING OVER THE GENTLY ROLLING HILLS OF IRELAND AT SUNSET.
Peirce

LOOK AT THAT TECHNIQUE! RUSTY SIENNA IS THE GREATEST PAINTER IN THE WORLD TODAY!

THEN WHAT'S HE DOING HOSTING A CHEESY TV SHOW? WHY ISN'T HE IN A MUSEUM OR SOME-THING?
LOOK, TEDDY, DON'T ASK ME TO EX-PLAIN THE AB-SURDITIES OF THE ART WORLD!

ALL I KNOW IS: WHEN RUSTY PAINTS A LAKE, IT LOOKS LIKE A LAKE! WHEN HE PAINTS A TREE, IT LOOKS LIKE A TREE! WHEN HE PAINTS AN ALP, IT LOOKS LIKE AN ALP!

"AN ALP"?
YOU CAN TELL IT'S AN ALP BECAUSE OF THE SHEP-HERD GIRL IN THE CORNER.
Peirce

C'MON, NATE, LET'S SHOOT SOME HOOPS.
NOT YET. RUSTY HASN'T FINISHED THE PAINTING YET.

THE SHOW ENDS IN TWO MINUTES, DUDE. HE LOOKS DONE TO ME.
NO, NO... THE PART THAT SHOWS WHAT A GENIUS HE IS COMES AT THE END.

...AND HEY, KNOW WHAT I'M GOING TO DO NEXT, JUST FOR FUN? I'M GOING TO ADD A COUPLE OF DUCKS!

SEE?
I KNOW, I KNOW! CALL ME ZANY!
Peirce

WHAT'S UP?
I JUST GOOGLED RUSTY SIENNA! I'M THINKING OF SENDING HIM A FAN LETTER!

LET'S SEE..."RUSTY SIENNA, AMERICA'S FAVORITE TELEVISION ARTIST... BLAH BLAH BLAH... BORN APRIL 28TH, 1940..."

"DIED MAY 7TH, 1996."

WHAT?!
YOU KNOW, I **THOUGHT** HE LOOKED KIND OF PALE.
Peirce

WHAT THE...? RUSTY SIENNA IS DEAD? HE'S DEAD?
YUP, ACCORDING TO THIS WEB SITE.

BUT!... THE GUY'S ON TV EVERY DAY!
UH, HELLO? EVER HEAR OF RERUNS?

SO... ALL THOSE PAINTINGS HE DOES... THOSE ARE RERUNS? THOSE ARE, LIKE... TWENTY YEARS OLD?
GUESS SO.

BUT... THEY SEEM SO FRESH AND CONTEMPORARY!
YES, THEY DO HAVE THAT QUALITY.
Peirce

I CAN'T **BELIEVE** THIS NEWS ABOUT RUSTY SIENNA! I'M IN **SHOCK**!

IT SAYS HERE HE DIED WHILE TAPING HIS TV SHOW, "OIL PAINTING WITH RUSTY," BACK IN 1996.

SO THE MAN I'VE IDOLIZED FOR MY WHOLE LIFE HAS BEEN SECRETLY **DEAD** THE ENTIRE TIME?

"SECRETLY DEAD"?
ACTUALLY, LET'S NOT THINK OF HIM AS "DEAD." LET'S THINK OF HIM AS "TIMELESS."
Peirce

HERE YA GO, KID.
THANKS!
SLUP!

NO, SPITSY! BACK OFF! THIS IS MINE!
WURF!

I SAID NO, YOU FLEABAG! I'M NOT SHARING MY ICE CREAM!

AND DON'T ASK ME TO BUY YOU ONE OF YOUR OWN, EITHER! I'M OUT OF MONEY!
WOORF?

WHIMPER...
SIGH...

ALL RIGHT, ALL RIGHT... GIVE ME THAT TENNIS BALL.

FRANCIS.
HM?

CATCH.
GAH!

DON'T SAY I NEVER DO ANYTHING NICE FOR YOU.
SLORPF
SLORPF
SLORPF
SLORPF
SLORPF

DAD, THE 10K IS ONLY A FEW DAYS AWAY! SHOULDN'T YOU BE TRAINING?
NOT NECES-SARILY.

ACCORDING TO ALL THE RUNNING MAGAZINES, YOU'RE SUPPOSED TO "TAPER"! YOU TRAIN LESS AS YOU GET CLOSER TO THE RACE!

IT'S IMPORTANT NOT TO OVERDO IT.

TO OVERDO SOMETHING, YOU'VE GOT TO HAVE DONE IT IN THE FIRST PLACE.
CAN YOU GET ME SOMETHING TO WASH DOWN THESE CHIPS?
Peirce

DAD, LET ME GIVE IT TO YOU STRAIGHT: I'M NOT SURE YOU'RE READY TO RUN A 10K.
OH, COME ON, NATE!

YOU ACT AS IF I'M TOTALLY INEXPERIENCED! I'LL HAVE YOU KNOW THAT I WAS A MEMBER OF MY HIGH SCHOOL TRACK TEAM!

YEAH, I KNEW THAT.
YOU DID?
I'VE SEEN YOUR YEARBOOK.
YOU HAVE?

HE WAS THE EQUIPMENT MANAGER.
BUSTED.
Peirce

GASP! HOW'D I DO?
TWENTY MINUTES ON THE DOT.
WRIGHT

WHAT? BUT I WAS AT THE HALFWAY POINT IN ONLY **EIGHT** MINUTES!

WHY WAS MY SECOND HALF SO MUCH SLOWER?

COULD IT HAVE BEEN YOUR PIT STOP AT "STAR-BUCKS"?
NO, NO... THERE WAS NO LINE.
Peirce

OKAY, THAT'S ENOUGH FOR TODAY.
BUT DAD! YOU STILL CAN'T RUN MORE THAN **TWO MILES!**

HOW DO YOU EXPECT TO DO THE FULL 10K ON RACE DAY?
SIMPLE! ADRENALINE!

ONCE THE ADRENALINE KICKS IN, I'LL MANAGE TEN KILOMETERS WITH **EASE!** AND PROBABLY AT A PRETTY FAST CLIP!

HE'S GIVING ENTIRELY NEW MEANING TO THE TERM "RUNNER'S HIGH."
Peirce

THAT... WOW!... THAT SEEMS LONGER THAN... I MEAN... I'VE DRIVEN THAT ROUTE AND IT'S PRETTY... UH... HOW FAR **IS** THAT, EXACTLY?

DAD, WHAT ARE YOU **DOING**?
CARBO LOADING!
MUNCH
SLURP

ACCORDING TO ALL THE ARTICLES, NOTHING BEATS A BIG PLATE OF PASTA FOR A PRE-RACE MEAL!

YOU'RE SUPPOSED TO CARBO LOAD THE **NIGHT BEFORE** YOU RUN!!
OH.

IT'S 7:00 A.M., DAD. YOUR RACE STARTS IN AN HOUR.
EXACTLY. SO I'M TRYING TO EAT FAST.
NARF
NARF

ARRGH!
WHAT'S UP, DAD?

I'VE BEEN TRYING TO FIGURE OUT THIS BRAIN TEASER FOR AN **HOUR**!

MAY I ?
BE MY GUEST. IT'S **IMPOSSIBLE**!
MM.... MMM HMM...

GOT IT. THE SISTERS WERE BORN IN THIS ORDER: ELEANOR, EILEEN, ELIZABETH, EMILY AND EVELYN.

THAT WAS THE EASIEST BRAIN TEASER I'VE EVER SEEN.

THE PROBLEM WITH TEASING IS THAT IT OFTEN LEADS TO OUTRIGHT HUMILIATION.
Peirce

THE RACE STARTS IN FIVE MINUTES!... I'M GETTING A LITTLE NERVOUS.
DAD, DAD! RELAX!
401
330

REMEMBER: IT'LL ONLY LAST AN HOUR, AND THEN IT'LL BE OVER!

ACTUALLY, YOU'RE PRETTY SLOW... SO MAYBE IT'LL LAST AN HOUR AND A HALF.
401

YOU KNOW WHAT? TO BE SAFE, LET'S SAY TWO HOURS.
THANKS FOR YOUR SUPPORT.
Peirce

LINE UP, RUNNERS!
THIS IS MY FIRST 10 K.
OH, REALLY? YOU'LL **LOVE** IT! IT'S TRE**MEN**DOUS!
40
173

I'VE RUN THIS COURSE MANY TIMES, AND IT'S **BRUTAL**! IT'S **PUNISHING**! THAT'S WHY YOU'LL **LOVE** IT!

LAST YEAR I PUKED MY GUTS OUT ON THE HILLS AND **STILL** RAN A PERSONAL BEST! **THAT**, MY FRIEND, IS WHY WE **RUN**!
40
173

IT IS?
SHAKE HANDS WITH THE **PAIN**!
40
Peirce

BANG!
THERE'S THE GUN! I'LL START OUT SLOW FOR THE FIRST MILE OR TWO...

PHEW! THIS ROAD DOESN'T REALLY **LOOK** UPHILL, BUT IT SURE **FEELS** UPHILL!

GASP!... I SEE SOMETHING UP AHEAD! MAYBE IT'S... COULD IT BE...?

IS THIS A WATER STOP?
THIS IS THE STARTING LINE.
VOLUNTEER
10K
peirce

GASP! WHEEZE!
HEY! DOIN' GREAT, PAL!
VOLUNTEER

PANT! WHAT DO YOU HAVE?
WATER AND WET SPONGES.

OH.

NO SAND-WICHES?
SORRY, MAN. BUT THEY'VE GOT BANANAS AT THE FIN-ISH LINE.

GASP! ... I'M COOKED! I'M NOT SURE I CAN KEEP GOING! ... I.... I....
7K

?... WHAT'S THIS?... THIS GUY WHO'S COMING UP BEHIND ME LOOKS ABOUT EIGHTY YEARS OLD!

I CAN'T LET MYSELF GET PASSED BY SOMEBODY TWICE MY AGE! I CAN'T!... I WON'T!

YES, I WILL.
COMIN' THROUGH, SONNY!

GO, DAD, GO! FINISH STRONG! YES!!

I MADE IT! GASP! I DID IT!
GREAT JOB, DAD!

...AND I DIDN'T FINISH LAST! DID YOU SEE ME PASS THOSE TWO LADIES IN THE HOME STRETCH?
UH... YEAH! YES!
401

THEY WEREN'T IN THE RACE, WERE THEY?
NO, THEY WERE WALK-ING THEIR DOGS. BUT YOU BLEW BY THEM!
401
Peirce

WANT TO KNOW, ONCE AND FOR ALL, WHY CATS ARE BETTER THAN DOGS?
NOT REALLY.

THEY'RE MORE AGILE! COMPARED TO CATS, DOGS ARE SLOW AND CLUMSY!

HERE'S AN EXAMPLE: IF YOU DROPPED A CAT UPSIDE DOWN FROM A SECOND-FLOOR WINDOW, WHAT WOULD HAPPEN?
IT WOULD LAND ON ITS FEET!

NOW!... WHAT WOULD HAPPEN IF YOU DROPPED A DOG UPSIDE DOWN FROM THAT VERY SAME SECOND-FLOOR WINDOW?

IT WOULD LAND ON THE CAT.

HIGH FIVE!
THAT'S WHY YOU DROP THE CAT FIRST!
Peirce

WHAT ARE YOU DOING?
DIGGING UP MY TIME CAPSULE, FRANCIS!
CHOP CHOP CHOP CHOP CHOP CHOP

REMEMBER WHEN WE MADE TIME CAPSULES BACK IN THIRD GRADE? WELL, I BURIED MINE **RIGHT HERE!**
CHOP CHOP CHOP CHOP CHOP CHOP
CHUNK!

...OR IS THIS WHERE I BURIED MY HAMSTER?
EWW.
Peirce

WHERE **IS** IT? I REMEMBER BURYING MY TIME CAPSULE **RIGHT HERE!**
MAYBE YOUR MEMORY IS WRONG.

MY MEMORY IS **PERFECT!** I REMEMBER DIGGING FOR HOURS IN THE BLAZING SUN, AND IT WAS ALL DUSTY, AND I FOUND THIS LITTLE THING WITH INITIALS ON IT, AND...

DUDE, THAT WAS "HOLES." WE WATCHED IT AT MY HOUSE LAST WEEK.

WELL, THAT WOULD EXPLAIN THE PRESENCE OF JON VOIGHT.
HE'S EASILY CONFUSED.
Peirce

WAIT 'TIL I FIND MY TIME CAPSULE! MY BLUE RIBBON FROM THE PIE-EATING CONTEST IS IN THERE... THERE'S A TICKET STUB FROM A SOX-ORIOLES GAME...

THERE'S A HAIKU I WROTE IN SECOND GRADE... A PICTURE OF ME AND MY UNCLE DAVE...
IF YOU REMEMBER EVERYTHING THAT'S IN THERE, WHAT'S THE POINT OF DIGGING IT UP?

SHUT UP.
Peirce

HOW COME YOU DIDN'T MAKE A MAP TO RE-MIND YOURSELF WHERE YOU BURIED YOUR TIME CAPSULE?
I **DID** MAKE A MAP! I'M NOT AN **IDIOT**!

IT WAS A VERY **DETAILED** MAP! A VERY **EXACT** MAP!
SO WHERE IS IT?

INSIDE THE TIME CAPSULE.
CAN WE GO BACK TO THAT "I'M NOT AN IDIOT" PART?
peirce

JACKPOT! I KNEW IT WAS HERE! I FOUND MY TIME CAPSULE!

...AND... YES! THEY SURVIVED! THEY DIDN'T DECOMPOSE!

"CHEEZ DOODLES" CAN LAST FOR THREE YEARS BURIED IN A CIGAR BOX FOUR FEET UNDERGROUND!!
WANT ONE?

ONLY IF YOU ALSO BURIED SOME "PEPTO-BISMOL".
CRUNCH... A LITTLE BIT GRITTY, BUT STILL "PUFF-A-LICIOUS."
Peirce

I'M HEADING HOME.
WHAT? FRANCIS, WE HAVEN'T FINISHED LOOKING AT ALL THE STUFF IN MY TIME CAPSULE!

THOSE THINGS ARE ONLY THREE YEARS OLD! THEY HAVE NO HISTORICAL VALUE!
NO HISTORICAL VALUE? NO HISTORICAL VALUE?

WHAT ABOUT "FEMME FATALITY" # 64, WHERE SHE BATTLES THE MOLE PEOPLE OF VENTRIS-3?
FEMME FATAL

AS I SAID...
BUT THIS IS THE VERY FIRST ISSUE TO FEATURE HER LEOPARD-SKIN TUBE TOP!
Peirce

CALEB, MY YOUNG FRIEND! WANT TO BUY A CARICATURE?
WHAT ARE CARICA-TURES?
CARICATURES $1

YOU KNOW, CARTOONY PORTRAITS OF PEOPLE!
OOH! I'M PRETTY GOOD AT THAT MY-SELF!

HERE'S ONE OF MY SISTER RENATA...
....LUKE SKYWALKER WITH OBI-WAN KENOBI...
...AND HERE! JACK SPAR-ROW FROM "PIRATES OF THE CARIBBEAN"!
WELL...UH... KOFF!... THESE ARE OKAY, CALEB, BUT...

WOW, NATE! DID YOU DO THOSE?
! ! !
THEY'RE GOOD!

HOW MUCH FOR THE PIRATE?
CARICATURES $1

UHHH...
CARICATURES $1
CARICATURES $2.00
Peirce

SCHOOL STARTS IN EIGHT DAYS.
NO.

YEAH, IT DOES. ON SEP-TEMBER 4TH.
NO. NO. NO.

YES, IT...
NO! NO! NO! NO! NO! NO! NO!

THIS IS A NEW STRATEGY FOR YOU, ISN'T IT?
NO.
Peirce

HOWDY, GENTS!
HEY TEDDY.
NO.

"NO"?
HE'S UPSET ABOUT SOME-THING, AND HE'S HAVING SOME KIND OF BRAIN CRAMP. ALL HE CAN SAY IS "NO."
NO.

WHAT'S HE UPSET ABOUT?
I DON'T WANT TO SAY. I DON'T WANT HIM TO GET MORE FREAKED OUT.

DOES IT HAVE ANY-THING TO DO WITH SCHOO—
SSH!
NO! NO! NO! NO!

ANY PROGRESS?
NO.
NO.

FOR ALMOST FORTY-EIGHT HOURS, HE'S SAID NOTHING BUT THE WORD "NO."
NO NO NO NO NO NO

THIS IS EASILY THE MOST ANNOYING THING HE'S EVER DONE.
NO NO NO NO NO

WHAT ABOUT THE THREE WEEKS LAST YEAR HE INSISTED WE REFER TO HIM AS "N. DIDDY"?
OKAY, YOU'VE GOT ME THERE.
NO NO NO NO

HOW CAN WE MAKE HIM STOP?
LET'S TRY SOME AVERSION THERAPY.
NO NO NO NO
SNAP!

WHAT'S THAT?
WE MAKE HIM ASSOCIATE HIS BEHAVIOR WITH SOMETHING BAD HAPPENING.
NO NO NO NO

NO NO NO NO...
SWAT!

DIDN'T WORK.
GET ME A BIGGER STICK.
NO!
Peirce

HE STILL KEEPS SAYING "NO"! I CAN'T TAKE IT ANYMORE!
NO NO NO NO NO
YOU'RE SO NEG-ATIVE, TEDDY! LET'S HAVE FUN WITH IT!

"HAVE FUN WITH IT"?
NO NO NO NO
YEAH! LET'S HAVE... A BLAST!

BLAST!

WHAT ARE YOU DOING?
TRYING OUT MY NEW AIR HORN!
SAY, THAT WAS FUN!
Peirce

SO... YOU'RE BACK TO NORMAL.
YUP.
YOU'RE NOT CONSTANTLY SAYING "NO NO NO NO."
RIGHT.

YOU'RE NO LONGER IN DENIAL.
CORRECT.
YOU ACCEPT THE FACT THAT SCHOOL STARTS ON TUESDAY.
I DO.

YOU'RE FULLY PRE-PARED FOR ANOTHER 180 DAYS OF MRS. GODFREY.

NOW WHAT?
HE CAN'T STOP CRYING.
SNIFF!

GAAH!

WHAT IS IT, NATE?
OH, MAN! WHAT A **HORRIBLE** NIGHTMARE!

MRS. **GODFREY** WAS IN IT!... AND SHE WAS **LIVING** HERE IN OUR **HOUSE**, AND...

EASY, SON. YOU'RE STRESSED ABOUT SCHOOL STARTING UP AGAIN, THAT'S ALL.

TELL YOU WHAT: JUST RELAX, AND I'LL BRING YOU A MUG OF HOT COCOA!
OKAY. THANKS, DAD.

WE'RE OUT OF COCOA...

GAAH!
HOW ABOUT A NICE TALL GLASS OF ASPARAGUS JUICE?

The Monday known as Labor Day
Is cause for celebration;
A tribute to the efforts of
All those who've built this nation.

I say to you: enjoy yourself!
And seize the day, my friend.
For when tomorrow rolls around...

THEY'RE **ASSIGNING** US LOCKER PARTNERS THIS YEAR? WHAT WAS WRONG WITH LETTING US PICK OUR **OWN** LOCKER PARTNERS?
NATE, YOU'RE WITH AMANDA WOODCOCK.

WHO?
SHE MUST BE NEW.
...AND SHE'S YOUR LOCKER PARTNER, ACCORDING TO THE RULES.

WELL, RULES BE **HANGED!** SINCE WHEN DO I PAY ATTENTION TO THE **RULES** IN THIS...
HI, I'M AMANDA WOODCOCK.

THEN AGAIN, RULES ARE THE **BEDROCK** OF A WELL-ORDERED **SOCIETY!**
OH, BROTHER.
Peirce

SO! AMANDA! YOU MUST BE NEW HERE!
YEAH, MY PARENTS ARE IN THE ARMY, SO WE MOVE AROUND A LOT.

WELL, IF YOU HAVE ANY QUESTIONS, JUST ASK ME, YOUR TRUSTY LOCKER PARTNER!
I WILL! THANKS, NATE!

I... I'M LOCKER PARTNERS WITH A HOTTIE!
Peirce

I'M LOCKER PARTNERS WITH A HOTTIE!!
...AND WHAT A LUCKY, LUCKY GIRL SHE IS.
Cloud 9

I CAN'T **BELIEVE** I'M LOCKER PARTNERS WITH AMANDA! HOW LUCKY CAN I **GET**?!

SHARING A LOCKER MEANS I GET TO SEE HER SEVERAL TIMES EVERY DAY! WE'LL HANG OUT...GET TO KNOW EACH OTHER...
KLIK!

FOOM!
Peirce

HAVE YOU CON-SIDERED THE DOWN-SIDE?
WHAT DOWN-SIDE?

SHARING A LOCKER WITH AMANDA! TALK ABOUT A GOLDEN OPPORTUNITY!
IN WHAT WAY?

WELL, GENTS... DON'T YOU THINK THERE'S A GOOD POSSIBILITY THAT... ...AHEM!... A ROMANCE COULD BLOSSOM?
IT ALREADY HAS.

NUTS.
OH, WAIT. DID YOU MEAN A ROMANCE INVOLVING YOU?
PEIRCE

I'M SORRY, NATE, BUT I CAN'T BE LOCKER PARTNERS WITH YOU ANYMORE.
WHAT?

AFTER ONE DAY?
WELL, I'M GOING OUT WITH JEREMY NOW, AND HE FEELS WEIRD ABOUT ME LOCKERING WITH ANOTHER BOY.

SO... HE'S THREATENED BY ME?

GUYS! I'M A THREAT!
IN MANY, MANY WAYS.

RED SOX.
YANKEES.
RED SOX!
YANKEES!

RED SOX!
YANKEES!

HEY! MISTER!

RED SOX OR YANKEES?

WASHINGTON SENATORS, BY CRACKY!

"BY CRACKY"?
THAT'S OLD SCHOOL RIGHT THERE.

RRRRINNNGG!!
TAKE YOUR SEATS, PEOPLE. NATE, SPIT OUT THAT GUM.

DON'T JUST SPIT IT INTO THE CAN, FOR GOODNESS SAKE!! WRAP IT IN SOME PAPER FIRST!

NOT THAT PAPER! THAT'S MY ATTENDANCE SHEET!

IT'S ALMOST AS IF SUMMER VACATION NEVER EVEN HAPPENED!
OH, HOW I HATE HER.
Peirce

I **HATE** SOCIAL STUDIES! MRS. GOD-FREY IS SO...
NATE, I'VE TOLD YOU THIS BEFORE...

I WILL **NOT** DISCUSS OTHER TEACHERS WITH STUDENTS! THAT'S ALL THERE IS TO IT!

YOU DON'T HAVE TO DISCUSS HER. YOU JUST HAVE TO LISTEN TO **ME** DISCUSS HER!

OKAY. FIRST OF ALL, HER CLASSROOM SMELLS LIKE EGG SALAD...
Peirce

I WONDER IF MRS. GODFREY IS A JERK ALL THE TIME, OR ONLY DURING SCHOOL.
LET'S FIND OUT.

MR. ROSA, WHAT'S MRS. GODFREY LIKE OUT-SIDE OF SCHOOL?
SHE'S VERY NICE.

WHEN'S THE LAST TIME YOU SAW HER OUTSIDE SCHOOL?
UHH...

SHE'S A JERK ALL THE TIME.
peirce

DO YOU THINK TEACHERS EVER HANG OUT TOGETHER OUTSIDE OF SCHOOL?
WHY WOULDN'T THEY?

WELL, THEY PROBABLY GET **SICK** OF EACH OTHER, WORKING IN THE SAME BUILDING ALL YEAR LONG, RIGHT?

WHY HANG OUT WITH SOMEBODY YOU'RE **SICK** OF?

HARDY HAR HAR!
Peirce

MS. CLARKE, DO TEACHERS EVER HANG OUT TOGETHER AWAY FROM SCHOOL?
SURE! I DO, ANY-WAY!

REALLY? WITH WHO?
MRS. GODFREY, MOSTLY. SHE'S MY BEST FRIEND.

HA HA HA
HA HA HA HA HA
HA HA

TURNS OUT SHE WAS SERIOUS.
Peirce

MS. CLARKE JUST TOLD ME SHE AND MRS. GODFREY ARE **BEST FRIENDS!**
OH, YEAH. THEY'RE REAL CLOSE.

I SAW THEM RIDING LAST WEEK AT THE STABLES WHERE I TAKE LESSONS.
WAIT, WAIT. MRS. GODFREY RODE A **HORSE**?

IS THE HORSE OKAY?

APPARENTLY IT'S A CRIMINAL OFFENSE TO SHOW CONCERN FOR ANIMAL WELFARE.
PRINCIPAL

HI, MR. EUSTIS! WANT YOUR LEAVES RAKED?
STIS

LEAVES? NATE, THE LEAVES HAVEN'T EVEN FALLEN YET!
BUT WHEN THEY DO FALL, WILL YOU PAY ME TO RAKE THEM?

WELL, SURE, BUT...
EXCELLENT!

WHAT'S THAT?
iPOD

HEAD-PHONES...

...AND CRANK IT UP!
ZWIK!

FOOM!

HEAVY METAL?
CLAY AIKEN!
Peirce

WE JUST SEEMED TO RUN OUT OF GAS AT THE END OF GAMES! WE WANT TO AVOID THAT **THIS** YEAR!

SO! THE TASK AT HAND, AS I UNDERSTAND IT, IS TO WHIP YOU MARSHMALLOWS INTO SHAPE!

THAT'LL TAKE WORK, SOLDIERS! LOTS OF WORK! BUT JUST REMEMBER THIS:

"THAT WHICH DOES NOT KILL ME MAKES ME STRONGER"!!

SO HE'S ONLY GOING TO ALMOST KILL US?
GULP!
FIRST RULE: IF YOU'RE GOING TO TOSS YOUR COOKIES, DO IT ON THE SIDELINES!
Peirce

LINE UP FOR WIND SPRINTS, SOLDIERS!
CLAP CLAP
UH... COACH JOHN?

I'M THE GOALIE, AND... UH... WELL, A GOALIE PRETTY MUCH STANDS AROUND MOST OF THE GAME...

I MEAN, THERE'S REALLY NO REASON FOR ME TO DO WIND SPRINTS, BECAUSE... UH... WELL, AS I SAID...

LIFT UP THOSE KNEES, NANCIES!
NICE TRY.
SHUT UP.

WHY DO WE RUN? TO GET STRONG!

WHY DO WE GET STRONG? TO PLAY SOCCER!!

WHY DO WE PLAY SOCCER?

TO... GASP!... HAVE... WHEEZ!... FUN.
OOLP!
WHAT'S WRONG, SONNY? LOSE YOUR WALLET?
PANT PANT PANT PANT PANT
SH
peirce

AWRIGHT, I'M NOT DEAF, CAMPERS! I CAN HEAR YOU WHINING!

"WHY IS COACH JOHN MAKING US WORK SO HARD?" WELL, I'LL TELL YOU WHY I MAKE YOU WORK SO HARD!...

COACH JOHN?... I FEEL A LITTLE DIZZY...
YEAH, YEAH. HANG ON, KID.

...BECAUSE I CARE!
FLUMP!!
Peirce

HANG IN THERE, GUYS! I KNOW COACH JOHN IS A BIT OF A TASK-MASTER, BUT HAVING HIM HELP OUT WILL PAY BIG DIVIDENDS!
GASP!
WHEW!
COACH

DID I EVER TELL YOU HE WAS MY COACH BACK IN HIGH SCHOOL? HE WAS HIRED RIGHT BEFORE MY SENIOR YEAR, AND WHAT A YEAR THAT WAS!

INSTEAD OF LOSING ALL TEN OF OUR GAMES, WE ONLY LOST NINE!

THAT'S LAME-TASTIC!
OUR WIN WAS A FORFEIT, BUT WE FELT GOOD ABOUT OURSELVES!
Peirce

I'LL COVER!
AND I'LL RUSH!

WHAT'S THE RUSH COUNT? FIVE MISSISSIPPI?
WHATEVER. DOESN'T MATTER.

DOESN'T MATTER?
RUSH WHENEVER YOU WANT.

THREE MISSISSIPPI, THEN!
SURE.
TWO MISSISSIPPI!
OKAY.

HIKE!

ONE MISSISSIPPI...

...TWO MISSISSIPPI!

GAH!
FSSST!

FLING!

MY MOM WAS THROWING OUT SOME PERFUME!
OOH! WHO SMELLS DREAMY?
Peirce

REMEMBER THAT BAND THAT PLAYED AT THE SPRING DANCE?
"THE DIS-TEMPERS"?
WHAT ABOUT THEM?

WELL, THEY WERE JUST A BUNCH OF HIGH SCHOOL KIDS, RIGHT? WHY COULDN'T WE DO THAT?

I COULD DO EVERYTHING THAT THEIR LEAD SINGER DID!
I TOTALLY AGREE!...

...ESPECIALLY THE PART WHERE HE SNEEZED DURING "STAIRWAY TO HEAVEN," THEN FELL OFF THE STAGE!
YEAH, THAT IS SO YOU!
Peirce

I'M SERIOUS, GUYS! WE SHOULD START A BAND!
WAIT, DIDN'T YOU SUGGEST THIS LAST YEAR?

THAT WAS JUST A VOCAL GROUP! I'M TALKING ABOUT A REAL ROCK 'N' ROLL BAND! WITH REAL INSTRUMENTS!
INSTRUMENTS?

YOU PLAY THE TROMBONE, I PLAY THE VIOLIN, AND TEDDY PLAYS THE OBOE!

THAT'S CALLED "ALT-ROCK"!
IF IT'LL HELP, I CAN BORROW MY DAD'S ACCORDION!

I'M NOT SURE I WANT TO START A BAND.
FRANCIS, **C'MON!** IT'LL BE **FUN!**

PLUS, WE'LL MAKE **MONEY!** THE SCHOOL PAYS BANDS **THREE HUNDRED BUCKS** FOR A TWO-HOUR DANCE!
WOW!

SO IF **WE** PLAYED A DANCE, WE'D EARN A HUNDRED BUCKS A**PIECE!**
WELL, NOT EXACTLY. AS LEAD SINGER, I'D GET A SMIDGE MORE.

DEFINE "SMIDGE."
LOOK, DON'T FORGET THE GROUPIES. GROUPIES ARE A **MAJOR** FRINGE BENEFIT!

SAY WE **DO** DECIDE TO START A BAND. HOW DO WE DO IT?
WE JUST... **DO** IT!

ALL WE HAVE TO DO IS SAY "WE'RE A BAND" AND WE'RE A BAND!
OKAY! WE'RE A **BAND!**

NOW WHAT?
THIS IS BORING.
PATIENCE, MEN. I'LL WHIP UP A PRESS RELEASE.
Peirce

NOW THAT WE'RE A BAND, WHAT SHOULD WE DO FIRST?
LET'S THINK UP A NAME!
HOLD ON, LADS.

AS LEAD SINGER, I GET TO THINK UP A NAME FOR OUR BAND, AND I'VE ALREADY COME UP WITH A GREAT ONE!

ENSLAVE THE MOLLUSK!

"ENSLAVE THE MOLLUSK"?
HOW COME YOU GET TO BE THE LEAD SINGER?
I'VE GOT THE BEST HAIR.
Peirce

"ENSLAVE THE MOLLUSK"? THAT'S THE NAME OF OUR BAND?
A GOOD NAME IS THE FIRST STEP TO STARDOM, TEDDY!

...AND THE SECOND STEP IS TO START PLAYING GIGS! THE MORE GIGS WE PLAY, THE MORE FAMOUS WE'LL GET!

GIGS?
GIGS!

JUST SAYING THE WORD "GIGS" MAKES ME FEEL LIKE A WORLD-CLASS CHEESE BALL.
CAN WE GO BACK TO THE PART WHERE YOU CALLED "ENSLAVE THE MOLLUSK" A GOOD NAME?
Peirce

DAD? THE GUYS AND I ARE STARTING A BAND...

...AND I WAS WONDERING IF I COULD BORROW YOUR GUITAR.
WELL, SURE! I'LL GO GET IT!

COOL! THANKS, DAD!
HANG ON! LET ME GET SOME OF THE DUST OFF!

THAT'S OKAY, YOU DON'T HAVE TO...
OH, I DON'T MIND! IT'S NO TROUBLE!

UH...GREAT. NOW CAN I...?
JUST A SEC. IT NEEDS TUNING!

I'LL DO THAT LATER! I'LL JUST...
NONSENSE! I CAN'T GIVE YOU A GUITAR THAT'S OUT OF TUNE!

BUT THE GUYS ARE WAITING FOR ME, AND...
E...A... D...G... HMM HMM...
PLINK
PLONK

TWO HOURS LATER...
HOW MANY ROADS MUST A MAN WALK DOWNN...?
CRIPES.
Peirce

PRETTY COOL, EH GUYS? MY DAD SAID WE COULD USE THE GARAGE FOR BAND PRACTICE!

SOON THE NEIGHBORHOOD WILL BE FILLED WITH THE SOUNDS OF "ENSLAVE THE MOLLUSK" PLAYING HEAD-BANGING, EARTH-SHATTERING ROCK!

WHO BROUGHT SOME MUSIC?
I DID! TWO SONGS!

MY "HOT CROSS BUNS" IS PRETTY GOOD, BUT MY "BAA BAA BLACK SHEEP" NEEDS A LITTLE WORK.
THAT'S GOOD TO KNOW.
Peirce

I BORROWED MY UNCLE'S GUITAR, AND HE SHOWED ME A FEW "POWER CHORDS"!
IT'S BEEN A YEAR SINCE I QUIT PIANO LESSONS, BUT I CAN STILL PLAY HALF-DECENT KEYBOARDS!

...AND I'M THE MAN ON THE MICROPHONE! THIS IS AWESOME, YOU GUYS! WE'RE A REAL LIVE BAND!

FOR THOSE ABOUT TO ROCK!.... WE SALUUUUTE YOUUU!

PERHAPS WE CAN SPECIALIZE IN INSTRU-MENTALS.
I WAS JUST THINKING THAT.

GUYS! HALLO!
ARTUR!
HEY, ARTUR.

WHAT IS ON GOING IN HERE? I WAS WALKING OUTSIDE, AND...
BAND PRACTICE! THIS IS OUR FIRST REHEARSAL!

AH. BAND PRACTICE. HOKAY.
Peirce

BUT... I HEARD PITIFUL HOWLING OF A WOUNDED ANIMAL.
THAT WAS NATE.
ExCUSE ME, THAT WAS MY FAL-SETTO!

SO! I WAS NOT KNOW YOU FELLOWS ARE A **BAND**!
"ENSLAVE THE MOLLUSK," ARTUR! WE'RE GOING TO BE **FAMOUS**!

WE'RE TRYING TO LEARN "I FOUGHT THE LAW."
AH! YES, THAT IS GOOD SONG!

BREAKIN' ROCKS IN THE HOT SUN... I FOUGHT THE LAW AND THE LAW WON...

YOU'RE **GOOD**!
YOU'RE FIRED.
WHAT?
Peirce

WHOA, WHOA! YOU WANT ARTUR TO BE LEAD SINGER INSTEAD OF ME?
NATE, ARTUR CAN REALLY SING! HE'LL MAKE US A BETTER BAND!

BUT THE WHOLE BAND THING WAS MY IDEA!
LISTEN, IT'S NOT LIKE WE'RE KICKING YOU OUT! YOU CAN STILL BE IN THE BAND!

HERE!

GREAT.
HEY! MR. TAMBOURINE MAN!
CHINKA
CHINKA
CHINKA
CHINKA
CHINKA
Peirce

SO LONGER, NATE. SEE YOU AT NEXT REHEARSAL.
BYE, ARTUR.

YOU ARE NOT UPSET THAT I AM NOW LEAD SINGER INSTEAD OF YOU?
NO, NO, YOU'RE BETTER. YOU DESERVE IT.

WE ARE STILL PALS, THEN!
STILL PALS.

OH, HOW I HATE HIM.
Peirce

THE "DARK SIDE," OBVIOUSLY, REFERS TO MRS. GODFREY'S SOUL. SHE HAS TURNED TO THE DARK SIDE AND EMBRACED EVIL AS A WAY OF LIFE.

THE MOON, LIKE MRS. GODFREY, IS HUGE, INHOSPITABLE AND DEVOID OF BEAUTY.

RRRINNNG!
C'MON, THERE'S THE SECOND BELL! WE'VE GOTTA GET TO HOMEROOM!
ONE MORE SHOT! PASS!

DUDE, WE'RE GONNA BE LATE.
JUST ONE MORE SHOT, TEDDY! GIMME THE BALL!

WONK!

GOOD TIMING!
THITH ITH TOTAWY YO FAULT.
REMEMBER!
TODAY IS *SCHOOL PICTURE DAY!*
PEIRCE

YOUR LIP'S ALL SWOLLEN.
I KNOW.

IT'S SCHOOL PICTURE DAY.
I KNOW.

YOU LOOK STUPID.
I KNOW!!
Peirce

HI, THKOO PICTHUH GUY.
EGAD, KID! SAY IT AIN'T SO!

I THOUGHT I'D SEEN IT ALL, BUT NEVER HAVE I LAID EYES ON SOMETHING LIKE THIS!

A SIXTH-GRADER RESORTING TO COLLAGEN INJECTIONS IN HIS LIPS!

I GOT HIT IN DA MOUF WIF A BATHKET-BAW!
A POX ON THIS BEAUTY-OBSESSED SOCIETY!
Peirce

I'M SURPRISED, KID, I REALLY AM. INJECTING YOUR LIPS WITH COLLAGEN AT **YOUR** AGE?

I DIDN'T INJECK MY WIPTH WIF COWAGEN!
HAVE THE COUNTLESS COSMETIC PROCEDURES OF SHOW BIZ LUMINARIES TAUGHT US **NOTH-ING?**

I DIDN'T INJECK MY WIPTH WIF COWAGEN!
MEG RYAN! LARA FLYNN BOYLE! AND OF COURSE **MELANIE GRIFFITH!**

MAYBE THE SWELLING WILL GO DOWN BY THE TIME HE SHUTS UP.
WHAT HAP-PENED TO THE SASSY YOUNG MINX FROM "WORKING GIRL"?
Peirce

KID, I KNOW YOU'RE A TAD BUMMED THAT YOU DON'T LOOK YOUR BEST ON SCHOOL PICTURE DAY... BUT THIS, TOO, SHALL PASS, MY FRIEND!

TAKE A LOOK AT THIS PHOTO FROM YEARS PAST! WHO COULD THIS AWK-WARD YOUNG MAN BE? WHO WOULD THIS SAD LITTLE BUTTERBALL WITH THE FRIZZY HAIR GROW UP TO BECOME?

THAT'TH YOU, DUDE.
NO! BELIEVE IT OR NOT, THAT'S ME!

WAIT... WHAT?
THITH ITHN'T HELPING.
Peirce

KID, I MIGHT BE ABLE TO MAKE THAT LIP A LITTLE LESS NOTICEABLE WITH SOME CREATIVE **LIGHTING**!

HOP UP ON THAT STOOL, AND I'LL SEE WHAT I CAN...
Peirce

OOPS!
BUMP!

HOW COME YOU GET TO BE NICKNAME CZAR?
HM?

I'M CHALLENGING YOU, NATE! I CAN COME UP WITH BETTER NICK-NAMES THAN YOU CAN!
WE'LL HAVE A CONTEST!

EACH OF YOU HAS TO COME UP WITH A NICKNAME ON THE SPOT FOR THE FIRST TEACHER WHO WALKS BY!
TEDDY AND I WILL JUDGE!

AND REMEMBER: A GOOD NICKNAME WORKS ON MANY LEVELS!
GUYS! COACH JOHN!
ACH

UMM... LET'S SEE HERE...
"FAST BREAK."

"FAST BREAK" IS A BASKETBALL TERM, WHICH IS OBVIOUSLY APPROPRIATE FOR COACH JOHN.
...BUT THE WORD "FAST" IS IRONIC, BECAUSE COACH JOHN IS SO SLOW.
ALSO, "FAST BREAK" IS A PLAY ON WORDS. WHEN YOU BREAK A FAST, YOU EAT. CLEARLY, COACH JOHN HAS BROKEN A FEW FASTS IN HIS DAY.

I KNOW WHEN I'M BEATEN.
LONG LIVE THE CZAR!
Peirce

WHA...? WHY ARE THEY PLAYING **THIS** SONG ON "OLDIES 98.9"?
BECAUSE IT'S AN OLDIE, I GUESS.

BUT THIS SONG CAME OUT IN, LIKE, **1982**! 1982 IS NOT THAT LONG AGO!
ONLY A QUARTER CENTURY.

CRUNCH!

DAD?
I JUST NEED TO LIE DOWN FOR A MINUTE.
Peirce

I CAN'T BELIEVE THE OLDIES STATION IS PLAYING **EIGHTIES** MUSIC!
WELL, HOW OLD DOES A SONG HAVE TO BE, TO BE AN OLDIE?

OLDER THAN **THAT!** I MEAN, AT LEAST GO BACK TO THE **SEVENTIES!**
SO "STAIRWAY TO HEAVEN" IS AN OLDIE?

YES.
"CROCODILE ROCK"?
UH... YES.
"MACHO MAN"?
NO. WELL, IT...
"BAD GIRLS"?
WAIT, I...
"WHAT A FOOL BELIEVES"?
WELL, IT... IT'S SORT OF...

I'M CONFUSED.
YEAH, THAT HAPPENS A LOT TO FOLKS YOUR AGE.
Peirce

HELLO, "OLDIES 98.9"? WHAT'S UP WITH YOU GUYS? YOU USED TO PLAY STUFF FROM THE SIXTIES AND SEVENTIES!

NOW YOU'RE PLAYING **CYNDI LAUPER** SONGS! CYNDI LAUPER IS **NOT** AN **OLDIE**!

UH... NO, I HAVEN'T SEEN HER LATELY.
THEY'VE GOT A POINT THERE.
peirce

WHAT DO YOU MEAN, "THAT'S **TOO** OLD"? LISTEN, YOU CAN'T... WHAT?... WHAT DOES IT MATTER HOW OLD **I** AM? LET ME TELL YOU SOMETHING, SONNY, I'M NOT... HELLO? **HELLO?**

YOU PROBABLY THINK I'M RIDICULOUS, GETTING SO WORKED UP ABOUT WHAT SONGS THEY PLAY ON "OLDIES 98.9."
NOT AT ALL.

IT JUST BUMS ME OUT THAT THEY'RE NO LONGER PLAYING THE STUFF THAT **I** THINK OF AS OLDIES!
I TOTALLY UNDERSTAND.

WHEN **YOU** HURT, **I** HURT!

DON'T PATRONIZE ME.
WHATEVER YOU SAY, DAD!
PAT! PAT!
Peirce

I'VE SWITCHED RADIO STATIONS! NO MORE OBSESSING OVER WHAT SONGS THEY SHOULD BE PLAYING ON "OLDIES 98.9"!

FROM NOW ON, I'M LISTENING TO "THE HAMMER 103.7"! THEY PLAY ONLY "CLASSIC ROCK"!

WHAT'S YOUR FAVORITE MOVIE?
I DUNNO.

YOU DON'T KNOW?
I HAVEN'T GIVEN IT MUCH THOUGHT.

WELL, WHAT ABOUT SONGS? WHAT'S YOUR FAVORITE SONG?
I LIKE LOTS OF SONGS.

BUT WHICH ONE DO YOU LIKE BEST?
I HAVE NO IDEA.

OKAY, THEN, COLORS! EVERYONE HAS A FAVORITE COLOR!
NOT ME.

OH, COME ON, FRANCIS! THERE'S GOT TO BE A COLOR YOU LIKE! JUST PICK ONE!

KLUNK!

SPLOOSH!

RED.
peirce

I WISH I HAD A MIDDLE NAME.

PLAIN OLD "NATE WRIGHT" IS SO **LAME**! A MIDDLE NAME WOULD MAKE IT SOUND SO MUCH **BETTER**!

WHAT'S **YOUR** MIDDLE NAME, FRANCIS?
"BUTTHURST"

SAY WHAT?
CAREFUL WHAT YOU WISH FOR.
PEIRCE

IS IT TRUE YOU DON'T HAVE A MIDDLE NAME?

YUP.
THAT'S WEIRD, DUDE.

WHAT'S YOURS?
√‾‾

THAT'S WEIRD, DUDE.
MY PARENTS ARE MATH TEACHERS.
Peirce

DAD, YOU KNOW HOW I DON'T HAVE A MIDDLE NAME?
MM.

WELL, CAN I THINK ONE UP FOR MYSELF?
MM.

I CAN?

WAIT!... WHAT?
"FUNKMEISTER"!
Peirce

GOOD NEWS, GUYS! MY DAD'S LETTING ME THINK UP A MIDDLE NAME FOR MYSELF!

I'M STILL MULLING IT OVER, BUT A CLEAR FRONT-RUNNER HAS EMERGED!
LET'S HEAR IT.

"MAXIMUS"!

VERY MODEST.
IS THAT A NAME OR A MALE ENHANCEMENT SUPPLEMENT?
Peirce

GUYS, HELP ME PICK OUT A GOOD MIDDLE NAME!

I'VE NARROWED IT DOWN TO CAESAR, SOLOMON, ARTHUR, ALEXANDER...

...AUGUSTUS, ZEUS, CONSTANTINE, HENRY, CHARLEMAGNE, AND JUSTINIAN!

I'M DETECTING A THEME.
EVER HEARD THE PHRASE, "NAPOLEON COMPLEX"?
OOH, NAPOLEON! THAT'S A GOOD ONE!

I'VE DECIDED TO STOP LOOKING FOR A MIDDLE NAME.

"NATE WRIGHT" IS A SIMPLE NAME, BUT SOMETIMES LESS IS MORE! SOMETIMES SIMPLE IS GOOD!

A SIMPLE NAME FOR A SIMPLE PERSON?

ExACTLY!
EXACTLY.
Peirce

YOU KNOW WHAT, TEDDY? FRANCIS DOESN'T HAVE A FAVORITE MOVIE.
YOU DON'T?
THAT'S WEIRD, DUDE.
THAT'S WHAT I SAID!
WHY IS THAT SO WEIRD?

MOST PEOPLE HAVE A FAVORITE MOVIE, THAT'S ALL.
EVERY-BODY DOES!
OKAY, OKAY! IF IT'S THAT IMPORTANT, I'LL PICK ONE!

MY FAVORITE MOVIE IS "CASABLANCA"! SATISFIED?

OH, YEAH! THE ONE WITH THOSE ZOO ANIMALS?
...AND THEY WIND UP IN AFRICA!
NO, NO, NO! THAT'S "MADAGASCAR"!

"CASABLANCA" IS A CLASSIC! THE AMERICAN FILM INSTI-TUTE RANKS IT THE SECOND GREATEST FILM OF ALL TIME!
HUH.
NEVER HEARD OF IT.

MY FAVORITE IS "DUMB AND DUMBER"!
HEY! SAME HERE!

REMEMBER HARRY'S BATHROOM SCENE?
HILARIOUS!
HERE'S LOOKING AT YOU, KID.
Peirce

DAD, IT'S ALMOST HALLOWEEN.
THAT'S RIGHT.

YOU'RE NOT GOING TO RUIN IT, ARE YOU? YOU'RE NOT GOING TO HAND OUT RICE CAKES OR TRAIL MIX OR...
RELAX, NATE! THIS YEAR I'M HANDING OUT SOMETHING SWEET!

SOMETHING SWEET?
SWEET AND HEALTHY!

PLEASE TELL ME YOU'RE NOT HANDING OUT RAISINS.
EVEN BETTER! PRUNES!
Peirce

DAD, NO! YOU CAN'T HAND OUT PRUNES FOR HAL-LOWEEN!
WHY NOT?

YOU'RE SUPPOSED TO HAND OUT CANDY!
PRUNES ARE NATURE'S CANDY!

PLUS, THEY HELP KEEP YOU REGULAR!
KEEP YOU...? DAD, NOBODY CARES ABOUT THAT!

YOUR DAY WILL COME, MY FRIEND.
"NICE COSTUMES, KIDS! SAY, HOW'S YOUR FIBER INTAKE?"
Peirce

TRICK OR...
NO! SSH! GUYS! GET OUT OF HERE!

HUH? BUT YOU DIDN'T...
LOOK, JUST TRUST ME, YOU DON'T WANT TO BE HERE, TURN AROUND AND...

OH HO! I THOUGHT I HEARD THE DOOR-BELL!

I TRIED TO WARN YOU.
PRUNES FOR EVERYONE!
Peirce

TRICK OR TREAT!
AH! ASK AND YOU SHALL RECEIVE, YOUNG LADY!

WAIT. WHAT ARE THOSE?
PRUNES! DELICIOUS AND NUTRITIOUS!

EW!

WAIT! THEY'RE PITTED!
I CAN'T TAKE IT.
Peirce

DAD, HAVE YOU EVER THOUGHT ABOUT HOW THIS AFFECTS **ME**?
HOW WHAT AFFECTS YOU?

THE WHOLE HALLOWEEN THING! EVERYBODY KNOWS THAT **MY DAD** IS THE NIMROD WHO HANDS OUT **PRUNES** TO TRICK-OR-TREATERS!

DO YOU HAVE ANY IDEA HOW EMBARRASSING THAT IS FOR ME?

DID YOU JUST CALL ME A NIMROD?
FIRE UP THE **SHAME-CAM**, FOLKS! I'M READY FOR MY **CLOSE-UP**!
Peirce

HOW GOES THE TRICK-OR-TREATING, DAD?
YOU WERE RIGHT.

KIDS DON'T WANT PRUNES FOR HALLOWEEN! WHAT WAS I THINKING, HANDING OUT PLAIN OL' **PRUNES**?

I **KNEW** I SHOULD HAVE GONE WITH THE YOGURT-COVERED ONES!
WELL, THERE'S ALWAYS NEXT YEAR.
Peirce

ALL RIGHT, SPITSY, PAY ATTENTION! I'M GOING TO TEACH YOU HOW A **REAL** DOG ACTS!
WAG WAG WAG

SEE THIS? **DOG!** THAT'S **YOU!**
WURF!

...AND THIS? **CAT!** THE **ENEMY!**

NOW **FOCUS**, SPITSY! DOG CHASES CAT! GET IT?

...AND **LOOK!** THERE GOES A REAL LIVE CAT!!

WHAT DO YOU DO, SPITSY? WHAT DO YOU DO?
! !

NAB!
ZIP!

WURF! WOOF WOORF! WURF!
Peirce

Check out these and other books from Andrews McMeel Publishing